www.marryAghost.com

By the same author

A Dilli-Mumbai ❤ 3 Story

Forthcoming title

The Unpromised

www.marryAghost.com

Abhimanyu Jha

Srishti
PUBLISHERS & DISTRIBUTORS

SRISHTI PUBLISHERS & DISTRIBUTORS
N-16, C. R. Park
New Delhi 110 019
editorial@srishtipublishers.com

First published by Srishti Publishers & Distributors in 2014

Copyright © Abhimanyu Jha, 2014

To my family for their love and guidance.

To friends who supported me during difficult times.

To all the ghosts of the world, anywhere and everywhere.

To people in search of their beloved.

Oh!
You cannot go without me…
I know you are tired, but come,
This is the way.

– Rumi

Are you searching for me? I am sitting next to you.
My shoulder is against yours.

– Kabir

Aaj jaane ki zidd na karo…

– Fayyaz Hashmi

Zindagi khatm bhi ho jaaye agar, na kabhi khatm ho
ulfat ka safar, Chalo dildar chalo…

– Kaif Bhopali

Bahut kathin hai dagar panghat ki, yeh ishq ishq hai
ishq ishq…

– Sahir Ludhianvi

Acknowledgments

I would like to thank the ghosts of the world for giving me the idea for this book.

I would like to thank my friend Mr. Ahlawat for the cover design of the book.

I would like to thank my family and numerous friends who faithfully responded to my questions on the best title, design, ending, etc., and helped me spread the word about this book.

And finally, I would like to thank team Srishti for helping me bring this book to the world.

Monday

VEERU:

Maahi. *The beloved.*

No… my beloved. My Maahi. I claim her for myself though she didn't return my love.

Does it matter?

Does it matter if the one you loved, loved someone else? Does it matter if you loved the spirit, not the body? Does it matter if you never touched the one you loved… because you couldn't? Does it matter if four days were all you got with her, *the four strangest days of my life*… perhaps of anyone's life?

It doesn't.

Where is she? That's the only thing I want to know now. But I fear to know, I shudder to know…

I don't know. *Where?*

1

Friday

MAAHI:

Where am I? What's happening? It hurts so bad. Why is it hurting so much? Please... please can someone help?

"Hello!" A voice calls me as a woman slowly walks out of the haze. She is a short old woman wearing black glasses and walking with a stick.

"I will help," she tells me when she is standing next to me. "Just hold my hand."

I look up at her. "Who are you?"

"A friend," she says. "You need me."

"What's your name?"

"I am Professor Deb Burman. What's yours?"

"I... I..."

"You have forgotten who you are, haven't you?"

"Yes! How do you know?"

"I know. I have been there. Here... hold my hand."

"But I can't get up!"

"You will. If you hold my hand."

I raise my hand to grasp hers, but my fingers pass through thin air.

I look at her in panic, but she gives me a reassuring smile. "It's ok. Let's try again. Something's happened to you. I know what."

2

Friday, Bangalore

VEERU:

It started with a bet between me and Jerry.

Jerry and I were a strange duo. We had met on a train, didn't know a thing about each other, and yet decided to start a company after talking for like... four hours. I worked for a mobile startup firm developing applications – the work far less fun than was promised. Jerry was in Oracle. He had chugged along for close to five years and was at the point where you begin to think if other guys with your profile and experience can become entrepreneurs and make shitloads of money, why can't *you*? In about a couple of hours, he figured I was smart, reliable and a risk-taker. In other words, 'entrepreneur material' (his words), and influenced me to think about starting a company.

To tell the truth, neither of us had a clue what we would do. We just wanted to do something fun. And make money. The dream of all entrepreneurs.

Soon, we found out entrepreneurship was less sexy than it was made out to be. I mean the first part, the 'fun' part, happened for a while. The second, the 'money' thingy: *never*.

After a bit of research, we started an e-commerce company, but couldn't influence anyone to invest in it. Quickly, we were at a stage where having exhausted our savings, we had to freelance to survive. And for some time now, freelancing had begun to consume most of our hours, replacing the e-commerce venture as the main job.

Not many days ago, Jerry and I had this extensive argument on paranormal existence. What else can you do when bored of both freelancing and an afternoon of trying to get your suppliers to give you bigger discounts?

I don't remember how it started. But as the debate went on, it was clear that Jerry was strongly ghost-positive; I, ghost-negative.

About an hour into the discussion, I was overwhelmed by Jerry's list of ghostly sightings around the world. I conceded that maybe spirits did exist given the number of haunted houses and castles, (and given Stephen King, Jerry added), but no way could they have memories and emotions.

"That's biologically impossible."

"Why?"

"Look dude…." I turned my chair around to face Jerry.

"Emotions are just chemical reactions induced by electrical signals created by nerves. You can't have electrical signals if you don't have nerves. You don't have nerves if you don't have a brain. And you don't have a brain if you are dead. Simple!"

But Jerry wasn't the one to give up easily. Abandoning the logical reasoning route, he started narrating a 'true' story his cousin had told him. In that story, a girl had committed suicide after being ditched by her lover, hounding her ex as a ghostly spirit night and day till he made her three promises.

Promise one: he would take care of her old mother, now alone in the world.

Promise two: he would bring a rajnigandha for her everyday, like he had promised her while wooing her.

"Rajnigandha?" I asked. "She ate rajnigandha?"

"Ha… ha… Very funny. There's a flower called rajnigandha also, remember?"

I grinned. "I remember."

"And you know the worst promise she rogered him into making?"

"What?" I asked, though I didn't see what was so bad about the first two promises. They made the ghost seem quite human.

"Made him promise he wouldn't love anyone else... he wouldn't marry anyone else…." Jerry shook his head, "…that he wouldn't even have sex with anyone!" he ended, revealing the *ultimate* tragedy that could befall a guy's life. He was almost mournful as he finished telling me about it.

It was an unbelievable story, interesting but unbelievable, though I appreciated the 'rajnigandha' touch. Funny too. I was quite struck by the ghost's insistence on her lover's sexual abstinence. Maybe it was tit-for-tat for having let her die a virgin.

I know it's not prudent to make fun of business partners, but Jerry was carrying such a bomb that I just couldn't help egging him on.

"You know," I told him, "This makes me think even ghosts should *date* other ghosts, consider taking them out for dinners or something. What do you think?"

"Huh?"

"Yes, think about it." I meant wouldn't that make the life of ghosts so much better? Dating and dinners could lead to less lonely and jealous, less vengeful ghosts. Bad for the Japanese film industry which excelled in vengeful ghosts, but good for the world at large.

Maybe if the girl in the story had found and dated another ghost, she would have stopped hounding the poor guy. He would still be having sex.

"Maybe," Jerry replied.

I looked at him. God! He was *still* serious!

I grinned at him. "Dude, I have an idea."

"What?"

"What do you think of making a dating site for ghosts?"

"What?"

"Yes!" I said, pretending to be excited. "Let's try it!"

I said it could even be a new business opportunity. An untapped consumer segment. What did he think? PlentyOfGhosts.com or GhostSaathi.com or even AajMereBhootKiShaadiHai.com?

We could even have a catchy tagline to attract the lonely, unhappy ghosts: *No need to haunt your ex anymore. Date dead people instead.* Or a shorter one: *I date dead people.*

Finally, Jerry got the idea that I wasn't serious.

"Don't tell me you are serious," he said.

"Of course I am!"

But saying that with a straight face was impossible. Not able to control myself, I burst into laughter. And my dear friend and business partner Mr Jerry Rajeshwaran, originally from God's own country, finally realized I was joking.

"You bastard!" he yelled at me, slightly pissed, and got back to his laptop after throwing an empty water bottle at me.

Surprisingly, from that day on, he was sensitive about the 'ghost' topic. I on my part seldom missed a chance of pulling his leg.

About a fortnight later, as part of our freelancing commitments, we had to spend three whole days finishing an outside project. We didn't get even an hour to spare for our own venture.

That forces entrepreneurs to wonder *what they are doing in life*. And that kind of wondering leads to frequent arguments with your partner about what's going wrong. Jerry thought it was our firm's strategic direction. But I thought our problem was smaller: our website. Developed on a regular platform with a complicated user interface, it was boring the hell out of people.

"So jazz it up then," Jerry said. "Make it sexy!"

I told him it was useless to improve our existing site. We needed to develop something from scratch.

He thought that will cost a hell lot of money.

"No, it won't. Not if we go the RoR/Scala way."

I didn't think myself an RoR expert for nothing.

"*Any* way buddy, it will cost plenty of money if we start from scratch. Unless you can do magic!"

"Maybe I *can* do magic!"

"Maybe I don't believe in magic."

"You believe in ghosts, dude! Why not magic?"

That was below the belt, but fair considering Jerry was being unnecessarily finicky.

"Don't you bloody go there man!" he howled. I chuckled. "I may believe in ghosts," he railed on, "I may believe in websites for ghosts, I may even believe in matrimony sites for ghosts, that's my problem! Don't make fun of me just like that! Ok?"

I was taken aback. "Ok…Ok." He was seldom so sensitive.

I tried to pacify him and told him I wouldn't go there, but seriously, I *could* make the website.

"Fine. Prove it!" he retorted. "And since we are on the topic of ghosts, go on… show me… make a site that even ghosts would like!"

His change of mind surprised me. I hadn't expected him to agree to it so easily. Teasing him about ghosts had worked. I made a mental note of that.

"Really? You are fine with me going ahead?" I asked, coz the site may not cost a bomb, but it will not come for free either."

Jerry shook his head. He said that's not what he meant. He meant I should design a dummy website, not the full version.

"Dummy?"

"Yup," he said, "a dummy. Doesn't need to be our website, just some dummy."

Something that would cost us nothing except my time. And yet convince him that I was right. "Just give me the bare bones of the girl… for free… and I will imagine the rest."

He grinned at me.

"Just get the basic architecture right so I can build on it with my imagination."

He grinned wider, outlining with his hands a curvaceous female.

I grinned back. "And you have that much imagination?"

"Oh! I have a *big* imagination, dude. I will make her a big girl, you will see." He winked. "Especially in the right places."

F**king sex maniac! He had to link everything to sex. I nodded laughing.

"Ok, got it. So how many days do I have to design the bare bones of this *girl*?"

"How many do you need?"

I shrugged. "Not many."

"Ok. God made a fully functioning female in a week… along with the rest of the universe. So, ten to design her bare bones?" Jerry said with raised eyebrows.

Was he challenging me? I think he was. I took the challenge.

"I am better than god, dude," I told him. "Three days," I said, "and I will make something that will have you *drooling*."

"Three days?" Jerry shook his head vigorously. "Don't think that's possible."

"Leave mission impossible to me," I said. "I am the one replacing Cruise in MI5."

Today was Friday. By Monday, he would have his curvaceous female. "And I will also put some flesh on her backend," I said grinning wide. "I know what gets your tongue lolling."

Jerry sniggered that he liked the frontend just as much; I better focus there as that's where my key expertise lay.

"But you know I still can't believe you," he went on. "Not questioning your calibre, but I just can't."

"Want to have a bet?"

So we had a bet. The stakes were simple. If Jerry won, I would do what Jerry said with regards to our strategic direction, plus give him a treat at Leela Palace. If he lost, I would have full freedom to do whatever I wanted with our fully functioning female; and of course, get the treat at Leela Palace.

"Cool man!" Jerry said giving me a thumbs up. He said he was looking forward to an interesting Monday. And the girl better be hot enough to get his imagination going.

I told him to trust me. She will… *sizzle*.

Saturday, Bangalore

MAAHI:

She is a kind woman. I can see that from her eyes that are most often hidden behind her black glasses. She sits across the verandah, waiting for me to speak. She is the only one who can hear me now, see me. She is the only one who I can talk to. She tells me not to fear her, that I am like her daughter, that she will do whatever she can to help me. I have begun to believe her now.

I wouldn't have feared her if it were not for the circumstances in which we met. In her big round spectacles, she is the kindest, most soft spoken professor I have seen.

She found me, I don't know how, when I was lost, dazed, scared, shivering, in unbearable pain, and took me in. I am indebted to her. Forever… if that word means anything.

Now she wants to know more about me, about my pain. How does it feel, she asks me.

How does it feel?

How does it feel?

Monday, Bangalore

VEERU:

Monday morning, Jerry asked me if I was ready. We hadn't met or talked for two days as I hadn't gone home, spending all the time in the office, even sleeping there. I asked him to wait till the afternoon.

In the afternoon, I motioned to him to step into my cubicle.

He came, turned to look at me, turned back to the laptop, turned towards me again, and said he was going to murder me and turn me into a ghost.

"Couldn't you make something else, you f**ker?" he complained the moment he saw the dummy website.

Which was quite expected; I had designed a site that was called *www.marryaghost.com*.

"A matrimonial site for ghosts! I mean come on man!" he said cribbing. "Do you have to pull my leg all the time?"

"Chill, dude!" I told him patting his shoulder. "Take it easy. Remember you were the one who challenged me to make a site that even ghosts would like?"

And anyway, wasn't the site like… so innovative? I could bet a million dollars there was nothing like this elsewhere in the world.

Yeah, Jerry shot back that I could certainly bet on that! Definitely there was no one as jobless as me in this world – arranging marriages for ghosts! And for my kind knowledge he had been joking when he had thrown that challenge, something which - thanks to my inability to understand sarcasm - I had obviously missed on Friday.

Then suddenly he noticed. "Don't tell me it's already gone live."

I shrugged, "It has."

"You really bought that domain name?" he said in sheer disbelief.

"Yep… GoDaddy it is."

"Bastard!" he exclaimed hitting me on the arm. How could I waste our hard earned money on jokes?

"Forget that… do you like it?" I asked him ignoring the jibe. I knew he didn't mean it. At least I hoped so. "Is it good?"

"It looks… quite good," he conceded. "Does it work?"

"Try it out for yourself."

"I can't, dude. I am *not* a ghost. And nor do have I any intentions of marrying one!"

I told him not to be such an ass.

"Have some imagination, dude! If not a ghost, you can at least be a vampire for a while."

"What vampire?"

"Dracula like vampire," I suggested. "Or like the *Twilight* one?" If he remembered, vampires were sexy, babes drooled over them, and they got to hypnotize and f**k any babe they wanted.

His eyes lit up. "Really? You can choose to be a vampire too?"

Keeping mum, I grinned and pointed at the heading that said "Profile Personal Details". And then at the second field where one had to select one's gender, "What do you think that is?"

The field read "Select Your Ghost Type".

"Cool man!" Jerry said clicking on the dropdown list. Then his eyes widened.

"There are so many types of ghosts!" he exclaimed. "I had no idea."

I told him he had 'no idea' about a lot of things.

"The girl you told me about… do you know what type of ghost she was?" I asked.

He shook his head.

"Mohini, she's a sexually frustrated female ghost who entices men with her beauty and then kills them. Check, I have put her in the list too."

Jerry looked impressed. The bugger really was a ghost aficionado.

"Wow, you seem like an expert on ghosts now," he said grinning. He began to scroll down the list. "Rest is good, but what the hell is a Banshee?"

"An Irish ghost," I said. "A real badass girl." She was supposed to scream so bad that she made you want to cover your ears and jump into the nearest well. And if you heard her scream, it meant someone in your family was about to kick the bucket. Fascinating creature, but not quite the one you would want to be around anytime.

"Sounds like my former boss in Oracle," Jerry replied, still fascinated by the ghost types and going through the list slowly. "My uncle died the day she first screamed at me."

It seemed I would have to *alphabetically* explain to him the types of ghosts he hadn't heard about; and he had just reached the letter 'B'. I was in no mood to do that. So I asked him if he could please choose his ghost type and start testing the website.

He shook his head, "I am a vampire, right?"

"I guess so."

"Why the hell do I need to marry then?" he asked grinning. "Especially when I can hypnotize and f**k any babe I want anyway?"

I was exasperated. "Ok!" I told him. "Don't marry."

Not that anybody was stopping him from being the playboy on a matrimony site, even if it was for ghosts. But would he please first fill all his details so we could start testing the damn thing!

"Don't get so bugged, dude," he said with a one-up expression, "I was just paying you back in your own coin."

He started filling the details. "I am a male... vampire... born in... Born in?" He looked at me.

I shrugged. "26th July... 1986?" That was his birthday.

"1986? So young?"

"What?"

"I have become a vampire, remember? Change of species demands a change of birthday, no?"

"So, you want to be older?"

"Of course! Aren't vampires like really really old?"

I shrugged. If that's what he wanted. "Ok... 26th July... 1947 then?"

"1947... just sixty-five years old!" He shook his head. "Tsk... even that's too young. I think I should be at least 300 years old to be a hit among the female vampires."

I shook my head too. Somebody was getting into the groove. He sounded as if he had sampled the whole vampire dating scene or something.

He put his year of birth as 1713 and smiled satisfactorily. Then he turned to look at me again. "I have a doubt, dude."

"What?"

"Is my birth year the year I was born as a human, or the year I became a vampire?" he asked with a totally serious expression.

"Seriously?"

"That's a genuine doubt man. Vampires will be confused. We must look at the site from the viewpoint of our customers."

Yeah… right!

"Feedback noted," I said with lips pursed.

"And that applies to other types of ghosts too."

"I will change "Date of Birth" to "Year You Became a Ghost". Will that solve the problem, sir?"

He nodded. "I have another doubt."

"What?"

"Are vampires born too, or are they only created by bites of other vampires? I mean does it ever happen… you know… that a male and a female vampire…?"

"F**k you, man!" I yelled at him, finally losing patience. "Can't you just fill the damned thing so we can start the testing?"

"Hey! Don't get pissed man!" he said with a wide grin. "I was just asking. It's a genuine doubt. I just want to know if I still have reproductive capacity left in me. I mean you know… post becoming a vampire."

To that I said even if he did have that capacity at present, he certainly wouldn't have it much longer if he continued with the level of his doubts. I was about to aim a solid kick at his reproductive organs if his horrible PJs didn't stop!

But despite my threat, my fellow entrepreneur's doubts didn't end there. After that, we discussed if ghosts were religious and believed in god (I told him in all probability they had their own religion and their god was a ghost or a vampire as the case may be); if vampires were open to inter-caste and inter-religious marriages (Jerry said he hoped it was so; it would probably be rather difficult for him to find a Mallu female vampire of his own caste and religion); and if as a vampire, he should be open to receiving promotional emails and SMSes.

"What are you going to advertise?" he asked licking his lips, "Sixteen-year-old virgins?"

"You wish, dude!"

"Can vampires register on DND?"

"Seriously, I am going *home!*"

Anyway, for all his jokes and leg pulling, Jerry was quite impressed after we had tested the whole website.

"You are a f**king genius, man!" he told me with genuine admiration in his voice. "I cannot imagine how you could pull off this whole thing in just three days. She's so damn good! A totally f**kable female. Take a bow."

"Her backend is quite flimsy though," I said, shrugging off some of the praise.

"Doesn't matter, dude. That's not your area of expertise anyway," he replied winking.

"So I win the bet?"

"Absolutely. She's all yours. Sex her up."

"You mean sex her sister up?"

His eyes lit up. "She has a sister too?"

"Our *own* website," I reminded him. "You forgot or what? The new one I am going to design."

"Oh yes," he said grinning. "Lucky bastard… Planning a threesome with sexy sisters now, are you?"

"Yeah," I said grinning back. "And I will need a lot of help with both the sisters' backend. You are invited to join in."

"A foursome! Ooh… sure. Count me in, dude! Count me in!"

MAAHI:

Dr Burman looks at the website and laughs. "What ridiculous conception of ghosts the living have!" she says shaking her head. "As if they were never human."

I look at the partially blind professor. "Are you able to see it?"

"Yes. I can see that much."

"You think they will help?"

She shrugs. "We have to try. We don't have much time left. Just nine days."

I can sense kindness in her unseeing eyes as she talks to me. And pity. I can't bear it and avert my gaze.

Nine days. *Nine* days when getting through one seems impossible. And *then*?

DAY 5

Tuesday, Bangalore

VEERU:

It was the biggest surprise I got in a long time.

Like any 'top management' of a startup company still looking for funding, my official mailbox was not chockfull of emails every morning I opened it. That was one of our dreams, by the way: to see the day when we would actually curse the volume of official emails we had to read in a day. So it was pretty easy for me to spot that *one* – completely unexpected, extremely strange – email among the few that lay unread in my Outlook that morning.

Someone had actually registered on www.marryaghost. com!

Bloody pranksters and spammers, I thought. Some people had no work at all. It was my fault anyway. I should have taken down the website yesterday.

Still, out of curiosity, I clicked on the mail.

The person who had registered on the site called herself Maahi Deb. She was apparently a female who was unaware of her ghost type, a twenty-five-year-old Indian from Bangalore, didn't know her religion, didn't know her caste, 5'6" in height, fair in complexion, loved fantasy, romance and mystery books, ghazals and outdoor sports, and was interested in marriage, long-term relationships and being buddies. She was also interested in receiving our monthly newsletter.

I laughed. Maahi Deb… nice name, buddy. I was pretty sure the person was *not* a female, *not* a ghost, hardly ever touched books, listened to Punjabi and Bhojpuri songs, and the only thing he was interested in was sex and wasting other people's time. I deleted the mail and started working, making a point in my mind to take the website down by evening.

I would have worked for about an hour when my Outlook showed another incoming mail. It was Maahi Deb again. She had emailed me at contact@marryAghost.com, which was linked by default to my official ID.

The subject line was "Please help" and the message read: "I need your help to find someone. Urgently. Can you call 7869914040? Please?"

Oh sure, that will definitely happen, I thought, and trashed the mail promptly. Some people, without doubt, were exceptionally jobless. Either that or they thought we were extremely dumb. The only thing I did in response to the mail was advance the time in my mind when I would take the website down, resolving to do that as soon as I finished working on the pitch I was making for a multi-branded toy distributor.

Fifteen minutes later, I got another email. Same person, same subject line, same message!

Unbelievable! Had I got a leech on my hands? I couldn't hold myself this time. Furious, I sent off a short reply blasting the person and asking him or her to bloody stop this practical joke and stop wasting my time. I had bloody work to do!

Didn't help. And if I had known that pranksters look for such kind of responses, and that it feeds their ego, I wouldn't have obliged. I got a reply from Ms Maahi in less than a minute.

She wrote back saying that she was not joking. "It's a matter of life and death. Please do call."

Life and death? Life and death, my foot! Wasn't she already *dead* anyway? I deleted her mail, again, and this time blocked her ID too:

maahideb3102@yahoo.co.in.

Curiously, even that didn't help; it seemed something was wrong with my Outlook. And for the next ten minutes or so, I kept receiving the same mail from her at the rate of 10-12 mails a minute.

I watched that in disbelief. I never had so many unread mails in my inbox since the day I became an entrepreneur. Now I was sure I had run into a mad woman, perhaps someone craving madly for attention (this couldn't be a scammer; scammers were definitely more intelligent). I closed my Outlook and spent the next few minutes taking the website down.

When the operation was complete, I shouted to Jerry to check whether he could still access www.marryAghost.com.

"K… will check," he yelled back. "Have you taken it down?"

"Yup."

"Why so soon? Weren't you planning to leave it up for some time?"

I was actually; the site was a matter of pride for me. Until, of course, I ran into this bloody Maahi Deb! I told Jerry I would explain everything in a minute, but I needed to confirm if he could still access it.

"Nopes," Jerry replied, "It's down, dude."

I breathed a sigh of relief. Then my friend got up and strolled up to me asking, "What happened?"

"Ran into a mad woman, or maybe a man posing as a mad woman," I told him, and then briefed him on what had happened.

He was incredulous. "Don't tell me!"

I nodded my head up and down ruefully, "Just my luck."

But Jerry being Jerry found something sexual even in that.

"Look at the bright side, dude," he said with his eyes shining. "She's crazy, she's wild. She could be a nympho! I think you should call her up on that number."

"Are you crazy?" I said.

For all we knew, she was actually a *he…* and he was a *gay* gangbanger!

Jerry nodded, saying he hadn't thought of that angle. "What are you going to do?"

I said, "Nothing, of course."

"What if she stalks you? Writes you a thousand heart-shaped letters? Sends you roses, chocolates, teddy bears? Shadows you around the city, her heart yearning, burning for a single look? Did you put our address up there?"

I told him to shut up.

"Ok. You want to go for a cup of tea and take your mind off the gay gangbanger?"

That sounded like a good idea.

Turned out it wasn't such a good idea after all. The tea took us around half an hour as we drank it leisurely. And when I came back and opened my Outlook, I couldn't believe my eyes. I must have received some five hundred emails in that half hour; all of them with the same subject line, from the same person, and I knew exactly what they contained.

And the bigger shock was how could all this happen when the website was down and I had delinked my official ID from contact@marryAghost.com?

Though it seemed close to impossible, I thought Jerry must not have checked properly and maybe I hadn't done my job right. So I checked again. I was right. The site was still up and running.

Jerry, the ass! Annoyed, I yelled at him asking if he couldn't do one thing properly!

"Why? What happened?"

"MarryAghost is still up, you f**ker! You told me it was down!"

He tilted his chair back to look at me. "Not possible dude. Checked it twice."

I told him to check it again. After a couple of minutes, Jerry yelled saying he had checked it *thrice* now. It was down. "Clear your cache and cookies dude," he said.

"What do you think?" I said. "Of course, I already did that!"

"What's the problem then?"

"Come here, I will show you the problem."

He got up and came to my cubicle. "Yeah?"

Opening my Outlook, I showed him. "*This* is the problem!"

"More mails?"

"Many many more."

"How many?"

"No less than some five hundred!"

He sighed. "Someone is really fascinated by you dude. Ok, let's do this again."

We checked *together*.

Site's disconnected from the host server –
check.

B).ht access code written to deny web access and return a '403-Forbidden' error – check.

C) All cache, cookies and history cleared – check.

We did the last check – we typed http://www.marryAghost.com in the address bar and hit 'Enter'.

Then we stared at my laptop with our mouths open.

The site was still running. Flawlessly. And the mails kept coming.

MAAHI:

I hate it. It's like asking for help by banging at someone's door repeatedly, even though they have already opened the door once and angrily told you to go away.

We have banged on the door more than five hundred times now. And yet the door has not opened again.

I am losing hope. I want to stop now. I feel tired. I want to let it be.

That's when Dr Burman calls me excitedly. "They have replied!"

I walk quickly to reach her side and read the e-mail. It says: "Who are you guys? How are you doing this? Is this some super duper hacking test?"

Hacking test? I almost have an urge to laugh. No, it's not a hacking test. Unless, it's about someone hacking my *heart* to pieces.

VEERU:

Astonished by what we saw, we mailed Maahi Deb asking if she belonged to some group of super duper hackers. I mean what had happened was totally puzzling; just didn't make sense. It was impossible from what we knew about web technology, and yet someone was doing it without breaking sweat.

We had automatically assumed while sending the mail that we were dealing with a group, that this couldn't be the work of a single person. I mean how was that possible? How could the site still run? Jerry said we were finally seeing real magic, and this time, I agreed.

We got a reply soon. No, they weren't hackers Maahi Deb said; or rather *she* wasn't a hacker. She was just someone who needed my help.

This mail was almost similar to the ones we had seen before, except this time it had some more information. I had been pleaded with to call a number; and the number I was pleaded to call, 9980******, apparently belonged to a professor from the Indian Institute of Science (IISc)– Dr Asmita Deb Burman.

"You may not believe me, but you will believe *her*," Maahi wrote. "She is an IISc professor of Molecular Biophysics."

I looked at Jerry. Calling a number couldn't cause much harm, I said. He agreed.

Dr Deb Burman picked up the phone after three rings.

"Hi, Dr Burman speaking."

I told her my name was Veerupakshya Mittal, and that I was calling about someone called Maahi Deb. "Did she—?"

"I know," she said interrupting me. "She needs you."

It was a deep voice – heavy, much heavier than the usual feminine voices, with a lot of bass. Measured and calm.

Assuring. I could picture a professorly, old woman in her fifties at the other end, used to giving orders. I could bet Dr Burman was feared by her students.

"Who is she? And why does she need me?"

"Those things can't be explained over *phone*, Veerupakshya. Come and see me. *Immediately.*"

Yes, I had guessed right; she was used to giving orders. And saying 'no' to her, saying that I wasn't convinced yet, that she should try to explain a bit more was difficult. It was not long since I had stopped being a student, and a professor could still get me to shut up even if I was unconvinced. So I agreed after she kept insisting that no more details were possible over the phone and that I shouldn't delay meeting her and Maahi.

"When are you coming?" she asked. "I am mailing you my address. I live at the faculty quarters."

"I will be there in the afternoon."

"Hurry, there isn't much time."

I said, "Okay, Ma'am."

"So?" Jerry asked once I had disconnected the phone.

I wasn't sure, I said, "The professor didn't explain anything. Just said Maahi needed my help and asked me to come immediately."

"Why do they need your help?"

"That's what I am saying dude… I don't know! She said it couldn't be explained over phone. I have to go, meet them."

"That's shady!"

"I know!"

"She really didn't explain anything?"

"NOTHING?"

F**k it then, Jerry told me. This was too shady. Magical websites, mysterious professors and a stalker called Maahi Deb. We never knew what trouble we could land in.

But I wasn't sure. "Umm, I think—"

Suddenly Jerry cut me short with a yell and an excited face, "Dude, what was the name of this professor again?"

I frowned at him, wondering why was he so excited.

"Asmita Deb Burman… if I am right."

"Yess! And what's the name of your stalker? Maahi Deb, right?"

I nodded. I couldn't see where he was going. And then I *could* see where he was going.

"Bet they are related," he concluded. "Mother and daughter… aunt and niece, anything. It's a family gang, I think."

We decided not to go to the professor's place and not pick up the phone if the lady called.

I was not at peace, though. The voice I had heard on the phone still bothered me. It was too calm, too straightforward, too purposeful to belong to a crook.

Crooks try to manipulate you, lure you in; they don't take a 'this needs to be done and you must do it' approach. No, the professor didn't seem like a crook.

I couldn't focus on my work the whole day. In the evening when I checked, the mails had stopped, though the site was still running. I went back home, thinking about the incident.

I wanted to figure out the mystery, and I couldn't. What was it? What had really happened?

I mean I hadn't got a call from the professor even though I hadn't gone to meet her like I had promised. It was the other way now: they were silent and I was anxious for some communication.

Later in the night, I couldn't stop myself. While Jerry was playing Road Rage, I mailed Maahi telling her that I was sorry, but I hadn't come because I was not sure of what to do after talking to Dr Burman. The whole thing was very strange for me, and I hoped she would understand.

I didn't know if I would get a reply, but I got one soon after. It was a short sad mail.

"I understand perfectly," Maahi wrote back. "And I am sorry for bothering you so much. I was desperate. But you will not hear from me again. Take care, Maahi."

I was numb for a few minutes; it was such an abrupt end to an unforgettable day. I mean, I was expecting a different kind of reply. Some kind of explanation on why I should go, or what help she needed.

But here, there was none. Instead, there was a simple and sincere apology. *I was desperate.*

And so it had ended just like that... our relationship. I mean it was a kind of relationship, right? Who else would you write more than five hundred mails in a day to!

I suddenly realized that I wanted to go and meet Maahi, explanation or no explanation.

Something was telling me she needed my help. Desperately.

Wednesday, Bangalore

VEERU:

I went to meet Dr Burman in the afternoon after Jerry had left for a meeting; I didn't want Jerry to know about it.

Dr Burman had already mailed me the address of her house. It was in Vigyanpura on New BEL Road.

To verify, I checked the IISc website and found that the place indeed housed the faculty quarters of the well-known institute.

I didn't call up Dr Burman before going. I knew that was risky, but I wanted to surprise her. If she was a crook, I didn't want to give her time for any preparation.

I called her up when I was about to enter Vigyanpura, telling her that I had official work in the vicinity so had decided to visit her. I would be there in ten minutes if she was home.

I heard a gentle but gruff laugh, "Yes, I am home. You can come."

Ok... My lie was as transparent as it could get, but what could I do!

Dr Deb Burman met me at the gate of her house. I had guessed right: she was in her late fifties. Physically she was unimposing: quite a few inches shorter than me with a roman nose, curly piled up hair, rounded face and chubby cheeks. She would have been pretty when she was young. And she looked different from what she sounded: less heavy, less professorial. Other than that, she wore black spectacles and carried a walking stick. Was she blind?

At her request, I unlatched the gate and entered the grounds. Not seeing (or perhaps ignoring) my hand that I had extended for a shake, she motioned me towards the small lawn surrounded by rose bushes, marigold and hibiscus shrubs. A table with snacks on it, surrounded by three chairs sat in the middle.

"It's a lovely afternoon, Veerupakshya," she said in her stentorian voice. "Shall we sit outside?"

I nodded. I doubt I could ever refuse a request uttered in *that* voice.

"Ma'am, you can call me Veeru," I told her as I settled myself in a chair.

She nodded, "Will do. And you can call me Asmi ma'am."

I nodded back and was thinking of picking up something to eat when Dr Burman thought it was perhaps time to unsettle me. You could guess that from the way her lips curled into a crooked smile before she walked up to me, put her hand on the back of my chair, and said:

"Now let me introduce you to my friend Maahi."

I was startled, "Maahi? Where?" I looked around the empty garden.

"Yes, Maahi. No need to look around, Veeru." Ma'am's smile got broader, "She is sitting right in front of you. On that chair."

She pointed towards it.

"What!" There was no one on that chair. Was she joking? If only I could see her eyes hidden behind the dark spectacles.

"Is that a joke?"

"Is it?"

"I can't see anyone!"

"Naturally."

"What do you mean naturally?"

"You are not supposed to be able to see a ghost... are you?"

Now she was *definitely* joking. "Maahi... is a *ghost*?"

"Yes," she said. "But I thought you already knew that, didn't you?"

"I knew that?"

"You made a site for ghosts, didn't you?"

I stayed silent. What could I say? No, I hadn't made a site for ghosts because I didn't know they existed.

After a brief paused she asked: "Are you scared?"

Was I scared? Was I really sitting in front of a ghost? Was there even a point in asking? Yes, I am scared. Definitely... a lot, my dear ma'am!

And was she speaking the truth by any chance? A ghost in front of me? A real *ghost* ghost? Those things that...

Unbidden, the image of the girl in *The Ring* rose in front of my eyes. The face covered by long, thick hair, the dripping clothes, crawling out of the tv...

Now I was *terrified*. I looked at the chair again. It was empty, just *empty*.

"You *are* scared," Dr Burman's voice was almost accusing as she sat on the chair next to me.

"A little," I said. "It's just that I have never met a ghost before." If she was telling the truth that is.

She smiled again, her crooked smile. "And I thought people who claimed to help ghosts find true love would do better than pee in their pants when they met one."

That surprised me. Did she really say that?

I was hurt by her sarcasm; it was unnecessarily harsh. A biting retort rose in my throat. But before I could voice it, something made Dr Burman look the other way – towards the empty chair. I stopped. It seemed she was listening to something...*someone*.

After about half a minute, she shook her head and said: "I am not angry... It's just that—"

Was she really responding to... Maahi?

Then stopping abruptly, she looked down. "Ok... Yes, I am angry. A little."

She raised her head and turned towards me.

"You know, if people really knew ghosts, they would be sad, not frightened when they met one. We are just a mess of unfulfilled wishes and dreams, unhealed wounds. Mostly harmless, except to ourselves."

"I am sorry."

"It's ok."

Then turning to look at the empty chair, she smiled a genuine smile for the first time since we had met. And I could see the lingering shadow of the once beautiful professor in that kind, radiant smile.

"Don't worry, I won't trouble your white knight again," she said to Maahi, her voice filling with affection. "He is safe with me."

She looked back at me, the smile making her look motherly despite the black goggles.

"See, the ghost you are afraid of is already trying to protect you."

I stared at the chair, trying hard to see the person who was trying to protect me. After the stare yielded nothing even after about ten seconds, I turned to look at Dr Burman.

She was still smiling at me. "I know you can't see her."

There was a disturbing pause before she resumed, "Anyway, meet Maahi, the loveliest ghost you will ever see, *if* you ever see."

I finally voiced the question that had been somersaulting in my head: "How can *you* see her when I can't even *hear* her?"

She smiled at me. "Let me ask you a question." The crooked smile had come back. "How was your website up even after…?" she trailed off.

"That was you!"

She nodded, "Who else?"

"But how did you—?"

She stopped me with a wave of her hand; said we didn't have time for those kind of questions.

"Maahi is in trouble. You need to help her."

In a moment, her face had turned serious and her voice urgent.

I looked at the chair. It stayed silent, and empty. I wished I could hear Maahi, see Maahi. Like Asmi ma'am could.

"What help does she want?"

"You need to help her find him."

MAAHI:

He has kind eyes too, like Asmi ma'am. But I can see he is frightened as he gazes at the chair on which I am sitting. Is he imagining what I am like? What is he imagining?

No, I don't want to think about it. When I was alive, I was told I was beautiful. What do I look like right now?

I don't know. I can see most of the rest of my body, which is fine, but there's no mirror that can show me what my face is like. Do I look ok? Do I look horrible, or frightening? I don't know.

Only Asmi ma'am can see me. She says from however much she can see that I am very pretty, but I don't know.

I don't want to frighten Veeru. I hope he stays. I hope…

"Maahi?" Asmi ma'am turns her head towards me and asks me. "Do you remember anything, anything at all?"

"No," I shake my head. "Nothing."

"Just the pain in the heart?"

"Just the pain in the heart."

"And yet you're sure he is there somewhere?"

I nod.

VEERU:

I was confused. What were they saying?

"Who are you talking about? *Who* is there… somewhere?"

"Someone very important," Asmi ma'am said. "But we don't know who."

"But then how—"

"First tell me… what do you know about ghosts, Veeru?"

"Umm, not much. A little bit, I guess…"

"Like?"

I hesitated to answer. "Uh, did some research on ghosts while making the website. That's how I know a little bit."

"And?"

Hello! Why was she pushing me like this? Did I ever claim to be a paranormal expert?

"I don't know too much," I said with some irritation. "While doing my research, I just found about the main types and how they got created and how they went about haunting people and how—"

"Could you get rid of them?"

"No ma'am!" I replied, waspishly this time. I was getting tired of her hostility.

"I didn't do that," I said. "At that point, I didn't even believe they existed, you see. All that I was doing was just for fun."

"So you read about ghosts just so you could make fun of them on your website?"

I was almost tempted to say with a sweet smile: "Yes, professor, that's it; you got it!" Let her deal with that.

But I bit my tongue and kept silent. I decided it was the best way forward with this inexplicably grouchy professor.

That's when the grouchy professor turned to the empty chair again.

"No, I am not bullying him," she said after listening for a few seconds. She paused to listen again. "Yes, I know he is a nice guy, but shouldn't one be more respectful towards things one doesn't know anything about?" She listened once more.

"It's infuriating when people think—" She stopped midway and listened for the third time.

"Ok…ok. Ya, I agree. He's kind enough to come and help us. I won't bully him," she said and smiled at Maahi. Her good-natured soft smile, not the crooked one she kept flashing at me.

She turned to me with the smile still on her face. I thanked Maahi in my mind.

"So you heard her… I am not supposed to bully you." Her face widened into a grin. "That's quite unlike my normal behaviour, actually. You look like a student, and I find it difficult not to bully students."

Ya, right! I could believe that.

"Ok… back to ghosts," the professor went on. "So now Veeru… let me tell you all that you should know about ghosts. Because what you read on the internet is all crap."

I shrugged. " I just took whatever I read on face value, and I didn't mean to—"

She interrupted, "I know you didn't mean to. But you did."

I sighed. By now, the professor had been scolded by Maahi for her unfriendly behaviour twice. And yet… old habits really died hard, I guess.

"Yes, I did… and then I made the website…" I reminded the professor gently. "And isn't that's how I am here?"

That caught her by surprise. For a few seconds, she was left without words.

"Yes…," she acknowledged after the brief pause, nodding her head slowly. "That's how you are here."

She turned to the chair. "I heard that chuckle, miss." She turned to me again, smiling her good smile.

"Smart, are you?"

I decided I would give it back to the professor whenever I could. "I hope my website looked like that," I shot back. "Smart!"

Asmi ma'am smiled in reply, first at the chair. "Don't be so happy," she said to the chair.

Then at me. "Yes, the site was… well done I should say…" She paused, then her smile widened, "But you'll have to try harder to impress ghosts. Let me tell you they are choosier than people."

"Are they?"

The professor nodded.

So I replied, "Makes sense, ma'am. They are more experienced than the living. They would choose wisely."

I added with a spark, "And isn't that why Maahi chose *me*?" I finished to hit the ball out of the grounds with panache.

MAAHI:

He is cute… and smart. Quite smart.

Though Asmi ma'am is very kind, she is not easy to talk to. I wouldn't have believed anyone this young could hold his ground with the forceful professor.

I am so, so glad that Veeru has agreed to help me. Though it's good he doesn't know that I didn't really choose him; I had no other choice.

VEERU:

"We have just eight days left to save Maahi," Asmi ma'am told me, asking me to concentrate. "That's the first thing you should know about ghosts. They need to find their way out into the oblivion within two weeks of death… or they may become trapped here, in an intensely painful state, for a very long time."

I looked at the empty chair. *I desperately need your help*, she had written.

"But how does one… I mean, a ghost… find its way out into the uh… oblivion?" I asked.

I paused, unsure if I should ask more right away, but still did, "Umm, and by the way, what's this oblivion thing if you don't mind me asking?"

"Oblivion? The best I can say… it's like a dreamless sleep for eternity. Like a nothingness forever."

I was surprised, "But why would you want that?"

"Why would you want that?" After a few thoughtful moments, the professor smiled a thin smile. "You do want that…Anyway, let's leave the 'why' part aside for now and focus on Maahi. She is in a lot of pain and trust me, she does want the oblivion."

I looked at the empty chair again. *She's in a lot of pain.* But how do you feel a lot of pain when you don't even have a body?

"It's like I have a hole where my heart once was. And the edges are burning."

I almost jumped up at the words. Did that voice – that soft, lilting voice – come from the empty chair?

The professor was laughing now.

"I can hear her!" I exclaimed to Asmi ma'am. "I can hear her. Is that… is that Maahi?"

The professor nodded, still chuckling.

"And she can read my mind?" I turned to the empty chair. "You can read my mind?"

There was silence for a few seconds. The chair didn't answer.

"Please tell me," I said cajoling the chair. "Really, I mean how can you…" I trailed off.

There was a pause for another couple of seconds. Then the soft voice answered: "No, I can't read your mind. It was just a guess. I looked at your eyes and felt that you were wondering about something like that. Wondering what my pain was like? So I answered."

"Are you in a lot of pain?"

She didn't answer and I began to think I shouldn't have asked that question. Maybe it was too personal.

"I am sorry if—"

"Yes, the pain is there," I could feel the sadness in her voice suddenly. The heavy weariness of unquenched pain.

"I wish I could be free of it. I wish I could go away like the others."

"I'll help you," the words came out of my mouth unbidden.

MAAHI:

I am so glad he is able to hear me, finally. Asmi ma'am had said it will happen; he will hear me. But first, he will have to believe that I exist. Believe that a ghost like me exists and needs his help. And now he believes I exist… I guess… I hope… I…

And he says he will help. There is a surety in his voice, a firmness of decision.

"What will I need to do to help Maahi find oblivion?" he asks Asmi ma'am.

"I told you. You will have to help her find him."

"Yes, I remember that. Him…" he paused, "who's there, somewhere, right?"

"Yes."

He shakes his head. "I know, ma'am, that this isn't a normal situation. But can we be like… more specific?"

"No. That's as specific as we can get."

"But—"

"The heart has its own reasons, Veeru, that the mind knows nothing of," the professor tells him. I have heard something similar before.

"Maahi's heart is deeply in love though her mind doesn't remember who he is."

He turns to me and asks: "We don't even have a name, Maahi?"

What do I say? That no, I don't have a name, I don't have a face, I don't even have a sliver of memory. Just the pain, just the yearning, just what is wholly unsayable.

And the certainty that he exists… somewhere.

VEERU:

Maahi told me she didn't have a name. No name, no place, no face. Absolutely nothing to find this Mr X who was there somewhere on this planet.

Now, that's definitely an easy task. Find Mr X amongst a billion people, even assuming X was in India. And if he was not in India…

"And why are we trying to find this… umm… guy, by the way? If you don't mind my asking?"

Maahi stayed silent. So Asmi ma'am answered me: "We don't know exactly, but we are guessing he was the… the one for her."

"The one?" Really!

Were we like in a Bollywood movie? Or in the *Matrix*?

Asmi ma'am agreed that it sounded over the top, but that's what she had guessed from what Maahi had told her. She was guessing that when Maahi died, she was with this guy, this unknown man whom she must have loved a lot, this… *one*. So what had trapped her on this earth and stopped her from finding her way out through the doors of the oblivion, was something which had to do with this guy. Something that would perhaps come back to Maahi when she sees him again.

So we had to help her find him, and then help her finish her unfinished business. Finish it before the next eight days were over.

Otherwise…

"She would be trapped here for a long time?"

"Yes."

"Any idea what this unfinished business could be?" I asked. "It could give us a lead."

However, I didn't voice aloud my actual thoughts. I mean, I was also thinking if the so-called 'one' was himself responsible for Maahi's death? Maybe, like so many Bollywood ghosts, the unfinished job keeping Maahi here was revenge?

It was Maahi who replied this time.

"I know what you are thinking, Veeru. But Asmi ma'am is not sure about that."

"Not sure about what?" ma'am asked Maahi.

"I guess Veeru is thinking if it was the guy whom I loved who killed me."

"Oh… that!" Asmi ma'am turned to me. "Yes, I have already thought in that direction."

But ma'am told me Maahi wasn't sure. She had talked a lot to Maahi and from what Maahi had told her, Maahi didn't have any anger or bitterness or vengeance in the feelings she had for this mysterious other. Just pain and yearning – intense pain and intense yearning, which didn't go with the murdered lover theory.

But of course, nothing could be said with absolute certainty. We had to be careful as we went searching for Maahi's lover.

"Don't worry," ma'am finished and her crooked smile came back. "You won't get into trouble during the search."

I didn't take her bait this time. "That's not what I am worried about, ma'am," I told her seriously. "I am worried how we will find in just eight days, in a country with a billion, this… this man with no name, this Mr X. How—"

"Mr X?"

I shrugged. "We have to name him *something*. Better than him being a man with no name."

The professor laughed in reply. "I know you are an excellent coder, Veeru, but everything in the world is not a variable."

She looked at Maahi. "Especially someone who is the love of Maahi's life! He's not a variable, he's a constant. We already have a nice name for him, don't we, Maahi?"

"Yes," Maahi replied after a few moments.

"Really? What's that name?" I asked.

"Hrithik," the professor said.

"Hrithik?" I was surprised. How did they know his name when they just said they didn't know anything about him? "How do you know that when—?"

The professor cut me, chuckling, "We don't *know* that," she said. "We made it up."

Hrithik, according to her, was currently the most handsome Bollywood heartthrob around town; and so the mystery man who we were about to chase, the apparent love of Maahi's life, had been christened Hrithik.

"Nice name, isn't it?" the professor asked.

If I was anywhere else, I would have rolled my eyes. For now, I let it be.

And why wasn't Maahi answering the questions instead of ma'am? Anyway, I decided to focus on the matter at hand: the identity and the whereabouts of Mr. Hrithik.

"Yes, nice name," I said. "But I had another idea, ma'am."

"What?"

I said, even if it wasn't Mr Hrithik who killed Maahi, what if they had both died together? What if it was someone else who killed them both? What if it was a case of star-crossed lovers – an unfinished love story? That could explain Maahi's intense pain and yearning.

"Could be," the professor said nodding. "Even I have thought about that. Fits. We will have to check."

I was excited. If this guess was true, finding Mr Hrithik would be quite easy. Even if Maahi didn't remember him, someone amongst her friends would definitely know who Hrithik was. "I think the best place to start is obviously Maahi's friends and family,"

I said. "I am sure that—,"

"Umm…," the professor cut me, *again*. "We have a problem there."

"What problem?"

"Uh… we don't know who Maahi's family and friends are."

I didn't get this. "Why? Has she forgotten that too?" I turned to look at the empty chair. "Don't tell me."

The professor nodded, "Yes… that too. She's forgotten everything."

"I am sorry," the chair said.

"But you do remember your name is Maahi, isn't it? Then—"

"No," the chair said. "I was given that name."

"Given that name?"

"Yes… like we gave the name Hrithik to the lover," the professor cut in. "She didn't remember anything when I found her. Just the intense pain and yearning for her lost love. So I gave her a name that suited her. Maahi. It means 'the beloved'. But she doesn't remember a thing."

"I am sorry," the chair said again, intense weariness permeating her voice. "I am sorry."

I sighed. And I had always thought *my* life was difficult.

MAAHI:

Why don't I remember anything? I see the disappointment on Veeru's face. I see him realize the enormity of the task of finding out who I am, who *he* is, when I can't be of any help. I am sorry, that's all I can tell him, I am sorry. I am sorry to be here, I am sorry for not knowing who I am, I am sorry to have asked your help, I am sorry to have put you in this situation. I am sorry.

I am sorry and I wish I could just disappear, dissolve into nothingness. Like the way I should have. Spare you the trouble and the pain. You and ma'am. But I can't. I am stuck. I am sorry.

I am sorry.

"You don't need to be sorry," Veeru tells me. "Why should you be sorry for loving someone so much? We will find a way."

VEERU:

I gave Maahi the assurance that we would find a way, but truly I hadn't got a freaking clue how we would do that. For god's sake, I couldn't even see her. I wish I could. At least I could try to guess her age then.

Suddenly I remembered something. "Maahi, how do you know you are twenty-five if you don't remember anything else?" I asked the empty chair. "I remember you filled that in the 'age' field on our website."

"Asmi ma'am guessed that from the way I look. She thinks I must be in my early or mid-twenties. So I put my age down as twenty-five."

I nodded as it made sense. I had forgotten Asmi ma'am could see Maahi even if I couldn't.

I turned to Asmi ma'am, "Did you guess anything else from her appearance?"

"Yes, she's very pretty."

I grinned, "Ok, anything else?"

"Her mom should have fed her more. If I was, I would have."

"And?"

"Long hair suits her."

"Ma'am!" I exclaimed. "Let's be serious, please."

I couldn't imagine the prickly, pugnacious professor indulging in such flippant humour.

"Serious? Ok, keep aside her appearance then," Asmi ma'am said. "Maahi does look like she's from the northern plains of India… but then the plains stretch from Bengal to Punjab."

So that was not a great help. And even the fact that she was from north India was a speculation; so we should forget her appearance and focus on better indicators of origin.

"Like?"

"Like the languages I speak," the empty chair said.

I turned to the chair. "The languages you speak?"

"Yes, they can give some clues to where I am from, right?"

Yes… right! Maahi was right! That should definitely give us clues as to where she was from. If she didn't speak many languages, that is. Hopefully, she didn't.

She did, as it turned out. At least, enough number of them to create another mystery. She spoke English and Hindi, obviously. Kannada too, along with a smattering of French. And then a little bit of Tamil. And then there was one more language she spoke which Asmi ma'am said she had discovered was a local language spoken in the state of Bihar: a language called Maithili.

Now *that* was interesting – an outlier. I was excited. "Maithili must be Maahi's mother-tongue then," I told Asmi ma'am. "Don't you think so?"

"Yes," Asmi ma'am said. "I think so too. And even Maahi thinks that's correct."

All of us had the same reason why Maithili could most probably be Maahi's mother tongue. If you moved around India and lived in different states at different times, it was possible for you to pick up the major languages. Like Marathi in Maharashtra and Kannada in Karnataka and Tamil in Tamil Nadu. But it was extremely unlikely you would pick up Maithili the same way, especially if you were as young as Maahi and therefore not likely to be a government official working with the locals in Bihar.

"So most likely, Maahi is from Bihar and has studied or lived in Maharashtra, Karnataka and Tamil Nadu," I contemplated.

"Yes… and we can even speculate that since I ran into her in Bangalore, this is where she was possibly living just before she died," Asmi ma'am said.

Now that was one area where I had to get more information from Asmi ma'am and Maahi. How had they met? Or rather, how had Asmi ma'am found Maahi after her death?

"So all we have to do now…" Asmi ma'am said with dry humour, "is search for a girl in her mid-twenties, belonging to Bihar and living in Bangalore, who died six days ago."

She smiled her crooked smile again.

"Shouldn't be difficult in eight days, isn't it? Especially if you consider that my guess that she is from Bangalore could be way off the mark and she could have lived anywhere in India?"

So we were back to square one. Or were we? Actually, I thought not.

If Asmi ma'am was right in speculating that Maahi was from Bangalore, I didn't think it was impossible to find out about her. It was certainly very difficult, especially within eight days, and would require a heavy-duty, meticulous search of all the hospitals in Bangalore on a war footing; but it wasn't impossible.

I was about to say that when Asmi ma'am shared another observation, taking us in a completely new direction.

"And also it seems Maahi didn't die in Bangalore." I was still wondering how she knew that, when she explained, "Because of the feeling of a crash, and the sound of waves nearby."

"Sound of waves?"

She told me, when she had found Maahi, she was in intense pain and disoriented. Very confused too, which was alright as that was a normal state for a ghost to be in right after a violent death. From Maahi's disjointed sentences, ma'am had inferred that Maahi had been in some sort of crash before she died; hard metal had hit hard metal. And just before her death, she had also heard the sound of splashing water nearby, something like waves crashing against rocks.

"Bangalore doesn't have waves crashing against rocks anywhere," ma'am said.

"Bangalore doesn't have that, but the waterfalls nearby, where we go on the weekends?" I suggested.

Chunchi Falls? Shivasamudram? Could Maahi have met with her accident near the waterfalls?

"You're smart," Asmi ma'am smiled at me. "Even I had similar thoughts, but I checked in the latest news thoroughly. There have been no accidents around the fall a week back."

So no, it wasn't the falls either and that left us with…

Nobody spoke for a while, lost in thinking of a place that fit the information we had. I hoped Maahi would say something, throw some new light on the matter, but she kept silent too.

So then I offered tentatively: Goa?

MAAHI:

How did I meet with an accident? Where did I die? In these puzzles lies the key that will unlock the doors of oblivion for me. Asmi ma'am says I was babbling incoherently about a crash and sound of waves when she found me. While I just remember waking up in front of a fog, waking up to a greyish, dense haze with small lights twinkling here and there. And being in pain. And being cold. And a woman walking slowly out of that fog and offering to help me. And then her extremely cold hand which I took time to get hold of.

And then I was here. Warm, though the pain remained, and intensified, slowly.

VEERU:

So Goa it was. We decided to begin our search for an accident that had taken the life of a beautiful girl in her mid-twenties in Goa. Maahi's death, from what it appeared, had happened in a crash near a water-body with waves splashing on the rocks – so most likely a sea. That's why I had suggested Goa; and Asmi ma'am agreed that it was the best place to begin our search. Ma'am said she had also already gathered from the internet a probable list of surnames of people who spoke the Maithili language; and armed with that list, we were going to scout the hospitals of Goa looking for a beautiful girl who had perished in what possibly was a vehicle accident on the 21st of July.

"We don't have much time," Asmi ma'am said. "Just seven days before all is lost. Today is already gone. But you guys must leave tomorrow morning at the earliest."

I nodded, "Yes, we will do that."

"Thanks," the empty chair said, the voice heavy with emotion.

I nodded again. I wish I could see Maahi, see the face behind the voice.

"Don't mention."

"I will get the tickets booked for the first flight to Goa tomorrow and…" Asmi ma'am turned to me, "Veeru, you will need to give me your bank account details. I will transfer some money to pay for the trip expenses, so you don't have to worry about anything."

"There's no need," I said protesting, though only half-heartedly. I wasn't flush with money.

"Don't unnecessarily play rich, Veeru!" Asmi ma'am scolded me. "I know you aren't."

She said she was rich even if I wasn't, and anyway, Maahi was now like the daughter she never had. It was her job to pay for the search, to pay for her daughter's happiness and so she would.

I nodded. "You don't have a daughter. You have a son?"

I wanted to know more about Asmi ma'am. Who was she, besides being a Molecular Biophysics professor? What about her family? Who were they? Where were they? Did they know about Maahi? Why wasn't Asmi ma'am asking them for help? How she could do all that she had done – like making my website run even after I had pulled it down and gather all that information from the news? I had a lot of questions in my mind.

But I got a crisp negative answer, "Now is not the time," she said. "After you help Maahi find the oblivion, I will tell you everything about me. Till then, let that be a mystery."

MAAHI:

We are going to Goa. Veeru and Asmi ma'am think that is where I died in a crash, somewhere close to the sea.

Goa. Is that where *he* is?

I hope so.

Then panic attacks me again. But what if we just met on a holiday, and he left after I died? What if along with me, he too…

VEERU:

"Dude," I told Jerry in the evening when he was back from his meeting, "I am taking a vacation for ten days."

"Vacation?"

"Yeah, Goa," I said. "Want to chill out a bit. Haven't done that for a long time."

I also told him that he need not worry about work, for I would keep the designing/coding work for the website on even while vacationing.

Jerry looked at me with a frown, "You want to chill out in Goa *without* me?"

To answer that was… difficult. Yes, why would you want to go to Goa alone and leave your best friend behind? I was left fumbling for words.

"You got a new girlfriend or something?"

"No, I—"

"Or you went to meet the IISc professor and her ghost?"

Was it that transparent? I guess it was. I kept silent.

"Dude, I warned you not to fall for their hoax," Jerry said with some asperity. "And yet you wasted a whole afternoon and went to meet them. And now they have convinced you to even go to Goa!"

I nodded. It seemed that telling the truth was the best option.

"I know it's a little strange," I said. "But I have to help the ghost Maahi find her lover. We have just seven days for that. It seems… uh… we think she died in Goa. And we are going there to find this unknown lover… most likely he was with her when she died. If we do that, she will find her release in something called umm… the oblivion. Otherwise, she will be trapped on earth as a ghost for god knows how much time. Being trapped here is a lot of pain, she says. If she doesn't find the oblivion, she's screwed."

"What?" Jerry asked. "You will help her find *what*?"

"Uh… something called… the oblivion."

"The oblivion?"

"Yes." I nodded. "It's like a… a…"

"Dude, did they give you ecstasy drug or something?" Jerry shouted, his face making it plain that he thought I had lost it. "What does that even mean?"

I sighed. "Actually, I did ask about the oblivion thingy. I asked the professor. According to her, it means nothingness. That's where we are supposed to go after we die… if we die well… and have no unfinished business on earth. And—"

"And have lost our minds! Dude, do you have any idea how crazy that sounds?"

"I know. But no more crazy than our website staying up and running flawlessly despite all that we did to take it down. Wasn't that crazy too?"

"Ok, that was a stinker, a total mystery," Jerry said nodding. "But then again, we also never know how far ahead technology can go without us knowing about it. This professor, whoever she is, seems to be some kind of tech wizard, that's all."

Yet that was different, he said. That was mind-blowing technology; not like mailing, seeing, helping, talking to ghosts!

Ghosts? Trapped on earth? Seeking oblivion? Did I see the *difference*?

And I thought Jerry was supposed to be the ghost-positive one among us. "But why would a tech wizard, someone who can do something we never saw before, something that almost looked magical, want to hoax, cheat us?" I asked. "Us?"

What did we have that was cheatable? A few paltry thousands in bank accounts? Shares of a company that could close down any time? Zilch intellectual property? What?

Jerry nodded. "I don't know, dude. It doesn't make sense. But…" He shrugged, "Fine. Up to you."

We left the matter there after our brief argument. Then we had a dinner of rice, dal and karele ki bhujiya, mostly in silence, post which we sat in front of our laptops to continue our work in the hall with the tv running at a low volume. Jerry plunked down on the bean bag while I took my usual position on the wooden chair-table as alternately Babli went on being badmash and Arnab Goswami and Barkha Dutt went on dissecting and analyzing the great Indian political tamasha. Some twenty minutes went by like this when suddenly Jerry piped up from his bean bag.

"Dude? Do you have a moment?"

"Yes, tell me."

"Isn't the full name of your professor—"

"*My* professor?"

"Ok. I mean *the* professor. Happy?"

"Ok."

"Ok… her full name is Asmita Deb Burman right?"

"Yes, that's what she said."

"Deb Burman… as in 'R.D. Burman' Deb Burman types?"

"I guess so."

"And she also said she was a Molecular Biophysics professor in IISc. Right?" he went on, glued to his laptop.

I nodded, "Yes."

"IISc as in Indian Institute of Science, Mathikere, Bangalore?"

"*Yes*! Where are you going with this?"

"Strange… because I am going through IISc Molecular Biophysics site," he said, "and there's no one named Asmita

Deb Burman in the Molecular Biophysics department of IISc. Neither among the faculty..." he paused, "nor among honorary professors..." he paused again, "nor among emeritus scientists..." he paused for the third time, "nor among technical officers and scientific assistants..." Another pause. "And finally not even among the office staff. Nowhere. Absolutely nowhere."

I kept sitting where I was.

He looked up from his laptop. "You don't want to come and check?"

"No. I should have done that earlier," I said. "There's no point now."

"There's a point. You are still here. Not in Goa. The non-existent professor has taken your time, nothing else."

"She took my bank account details."

"What? Really?"

"Yes."

"But why?"

"She said she would pay for the trip. Said she will transfer money in my account by tonight."

"Check your account, *now*!"

"But there's not much there. Why would—"

"We don't know man. Just check it!"

"Ok," I said and logged in to my bank website.

But it didn't make sense. I had some seventy-five thousand in my account, which was too small a sum for a tech wizard to go to such lengths to steal. And how would just getting my account details help her anyway?

I found with relief that everything was fine. My balance showed that all my money was still there in my account - safe and sound.

"Everything is still there," I told Jerry.

"Everything?" He sounded unconvinced.

"Everything."

"Ok…" Jerry said nodding. "Still you should talk to your bank tomorrow and let them know. And change your passwords for net-banking and credit cards and stuff."

"Will do that."

I didn't see much point, but I didn't want to argue with Jerry either. In a way he was right too; if Dr Deb Burman was indeed what she said she was, why wasn't she showing up on the Molecular Biophysics' department website?

I was truly bewildered. If she was genuine, why the absence from the website? And if the professor was a fake, what the hell had I seen at her house today? An empty chair talking to me? There was no doubt I had heard what I had heard. It's not like I had taken any hallucinogen before going to the professor's place, or drunk anything while I was there, so how come I was hallucinating if I was hallucinating?

Was the half-blind professor a magician or something? Had she like hypnotized me into hearing Maahi's voice? Or was she a master ventriloquist?

A tech wizard–cum-master ventriloquist? Now that would be too much.

And that voice from that empty chair. That soft, sweet, soul-touching voice. It couldn't be fake. I was sure she meant it when she said she needed help. *I wish I could be free of it, I wish I could go away like others.* Few things could have rung truer.

These questions kept going round and round in my mind till at about ten-fifty, late in the night, I received a text message from my bank. It said that a sum of 1,25,000 had been deposited into my account and my balance now stood around 200k. The professor had kept true to her word; she had deposited money into my account, not stolen from it.

A few minutes later, another message came, this time from the professor herself. She said she hoped that I had received the money transfer, and that she had booked the tickets for me and Maahi on the 7:30 am flight to Goa the next day and had mailed me its pdf file. She had also booked a prepaid cab for me at 5:00 am from my address in BTM layout to the airport; she and Maahi would meet me directly at the airport and she was really hoping that, as promised, I would be there for the journey to Goa.

I opened my mail account and checked. Yes, there was a mail from the professor to which was attached the pdf file of the ticket. Bangalore to Goa. 7:30 am.

What was I supposed to think now?

Thursday, Bangalore

VEERU:

I avoided waking Jerry up the next morning. Closing the doors of both Jerry's room and my own room and carefully maintaining as much silence as possible even with the presence of a pair of concrete walls between us, I went to the loo, brushed my teeth, didn't take a bath hoping a female ghost wouldn't mind it that much, threw my clothes and other necessary stuff into my travel bag, and went downstairs to wait for the taxi to the airport. It was 4:50 am.

The taxi arrived as scheduled and dropped a sleepy me to the airport at around 6:45. I went inside and looked around. I saw Asmi ma'am waiting for me near the third entrance to the foyer. She was standing alone looking in my direction, perhaps searching for me among the throng of people coming in. But it would have been impossible for the half-blind professor to see me at such a distance.

I began strolling towards her. As usual, I couldn't see Maahi, but I guessed she must be standing next to ma'am or somewhere close by.

When I got quite close to ma'am, she recognized me and waved at me. I waved back. Once I reached her, I said a chirpy 'good morning ma'am' with a smile and extended my hand for a shake that she ignored again. She just smiled back with an even chirpier 'Good morning'.

I grinned and shook my head; what was this peculiar aversion to handshakes?

I was about to ask her that question when her smile disappeared. She shook her head and inexplicably, a deep frown appeared on her face. Then all of a sudden, without telling why, she moved, crossed me, and started walking fast in the opposite direction – towards the exit of the airport which was banded on both sides by tin sheets, on the far side of which construction for the airport expansion was going on. For a half-blind person with a walking stick, she was rushing like hell to wherever she was going.

I was puzzled by the strangeness of her action. Where was she going? What was going on?

As she marched away, that's what I asked her – a little loudly so she could hear me above the din of the airport; and she stopped midway to turn around and signal me to shut my mouth. Then she signalled me once more; this time for me to follow her. She turned back to continue her frantic walking.

Surprised and puzzled, I followed her till both of us reached and finally stood at the back of a food kiosk now shut for renovation. I noticed it was a place safe from prying eyes, hidden as we were between the shut kiosk and the tin sheets. Very few people could see us standing there and that too with difficulty.

I started the conversation. "Ma'am, why are we—"

But I was cut off savagely, in a furious tone.

"What happened last night, Veeru?"

I was taken aback. "What?"

"I asked what happened last night?"

"Nothing. Why?"

Ignoring my question, ma'am continued in her enraged tone: "Don't lie to me! I know something happened. What happened?"

"I don't—"

"Do you know Maahi has been standing next to me all the time?"

I nodded. "Yes, I guessed..." I said tentatively. "But—"

"And do you also know she has greeted you three to four times since you came but you had no clue about that. None at all!"

"I didn't know—"

"Yes... you didn't! It was freaking obvious you didn't. But that's exactly my question. Why Veeru... why didn't you?"

I kept silent. Ma'am was bristling with rage. And my attempts at answering her, which she was anyway cutting woefully short, were not helping matters.

"Why can't you hear her anymore?" she went on in her fuming voice.

"Uh... I don't—"

"Yes, you don't! So let me tell you why. It's because there's some doubt in your mind now. You have stopped believing in Maahi's existence as strongly as needed. That's why you can't hear her anymore."

She paused for a moment and then went on in a calmer, but equally harsh tone. "And I want to know why. Why have you stopped believing in her? What happened last night?"

"Nothing happened last night… nothing, really!" I finally managed to complete a sentence. "It must be the time that—"

I couldn't manage to complete the second sentence. I was cut off again in the same dispassionate but grim voice. "Don't lie to me. I am not a fool."

It was clear there was no point hiding anything. I gave in. "We couldn't find you on the IISc website," I said.

There was a brief pause. Ma'am stared at me with piercing eyes.

"We?"

"Yup. Me… and Jerry."

"Why were you checking on me?"

Why? How could she even ask that? Like a thief taking a cop to task for trying to catch him!

"Because—"

"Because despite seeing what you saw yesterday, despite talking to Maahi, to… to an empty chair for more than two hours, you couldn't get over your scepticism about ghosts?"

I was cornered, so I hit back. "We thought you could have been hypnotizing me."

"Hypnotizing you?"

"Yes… we thought you could be a magician or a ventriloquist or something."

There was silence for another few moments. "Then why are you here Veeru?" Ma'am asked. "If you think I am a fraud, why are you here?"

That was a solid hook to my chin. I fumbled for an answer. "Because… I—"

"Because of the 125k that landed in your account last night?"

Her voice had become much quieter. I stayed silent. The truth was difficult to handle.

"I am sorry." That was the only thing I could say.

"Sorry is not—" Ma'am was not willing to stop ripping into me when for the first time that morning, I heard Maahi's soft, sweet, tinkling voice that came from my right like a saviour from nowhere in the cold, gray of the morning light.

"Ma'am, it's ok," she was saying. "Don't scold him. Almost everyone would have done the same thing."

And so, anxious beyond measure, I almost yelled the moment Maahi finished: "Ma'am! I can hear her again!"

I was so… so relieved to hear Maahi again. And so happy too. I was feeling like a total ass not moments ago.

Asmi ma'am turned to me and frowned. "You can?"

"Yes!" I tumbled my words out. "I heard… she just asked you to stop scolding me… Maahi… you did right, didn't you?"

"Yes, I did… I did!" Maahi said, even her voice pulsing with excitement. "Ma'am… yes he can hear me. He can hear me."

Ma'am snorted. "And just in time too."

She threw at me an almost disdainful look. Then she turned to Maahi. "Otherwise I wouldn't have let you go with him even to the airport entrance, forget Goa." She turned to me again. "Ever loved someone, mister?"

Where did *that* come from? And that was difficult to answer, so I stayed silent.

The professor frowned holding my face under brief scrutiny, then said: "Looks like you *did* love someone. And looks like it wasn't a great experience, was it?"

Staying silent wouldn't have helped, so I replied briefly, "No, it wasn't."

"She left you?"

"Ma'am," Maahi spoke softly, "*Don't!*"

Ma'am ignored her. "This is important, Maahi." She continued her charge of the love brigade at me. "So she ditched you and broke your heart and all that... and you stopped believing in love. That's what happened, right?"

"No," I replied briefly again. "That's not what happened. I still believe in love. But I did learn to be cautious." I emphasized on 'cautious'. "Being cautious is not bad. Helps you make the right choices, avoid tripping over bad ones."

"No, it's not bad," the professor nodded. "Not in many things. But in love?... I think not. Being cautious won't help you in love."

"How do you know?"

"I am old enough," she shot back with a half snort, half sigh that had a hint of sourness to it. "Even poppy old dowdy professors fall in love and have their hearts broken. But no matter what, believe and let go, come what may... that's how love works. Not by being cautious, not by being doubtful. No matter how much you've been hurt. Doubt... kills."

She paused for a couple of seconds. "It's the same with Maahi. She's like love. Forget that, she *is* love. Her name is love. If—"

"Ma'am... please!" Maahi cut in, "It's embarra—"

"Shush!" Ma'am continued to address me. "If you want to help her, you have to believe in her, in love, come what may. There's no space for any doubt. None." She paused again. "Do you get me? *None.*"

I nodded.

"I don't want what happened today happening again."

"It won't."

"Ever!"

"Got it!"

"I am a bloody half-blind old doddering woman, otherwise I would have gone with Maahi myself. But even if I am not going, I—"

"Yes Ma'am! I won't let you down."

"It's getting late, ma'am!" Maahi reminded us in between our intense conversation. "We have to check in or we—"

"Yes, a minute. Promise me you'll find her guy and get her out."

I nodded.

"Say it! Say the damn words, Veeru!"

"I promise."

MAAHI:

It's time to leave Asmi ma'am and Bangalore. I look at her, my saviour. An old, kind but determined woman. It was both surprising and heartening to see the way she took Veeru to task for disbelieving us. Poor guy; he was verbally beaten to pulp. I can't blame him for doubting us though; it must have been impossible for him to defend such a fantastic story from his friend.

An old, half-blind woman and an invisible ghost needing help to find a lost lover so the ghost can escape her earthly jail. What complete crap! More likely a sweet set of swindlers. I feel it was a miracle that Veeru even came.

He is so quiet after the verbal bashing he got from ma'am.

I wave to Asmi ma'am as I leave; I don't want to leave her. I feel like crying. Maybe I will never see her again. Never. This is the last goodbye to the woman who found me and sheltered and comforted me like she was my own mother. Helped me bear and get through my intense pain of the last seven days.

Suddenly, as the moment to pass through the door arrives, I am scared… terrified. Veeru goes through the security check, and is walking away through the hall inside, but I don't want to follow him. I don't want to leave ma'am.

I look at her and take a step towards her, but she shakes her head vigorously and stops me with a gesture of her hand. A mother leaving a toddler for her first day at school… no, for her last few days on earth. She signs at me to follow Veeru, and then suddenly, she turns back and begins to walk fast towards the exit. In a quarter of a minute, she disappears through the exit.

I am alone. I am terrified. I turn around; even Veeru is disappearing in the crowd of people far away inside the hall. Panicking, I run after Veeru through the space between a passenger and two security guards.

Nobody stops ghosts. Nobody asks for their identity.

VEERU:

I walked through the lobby towards the check-in counters thinking Maahi was following me. After reaching a spot a few meters away from the queues, away from the swarm of people and after looking around to make sure no one was watching, I called out softly to her to make sure she was with me. There was no response. I called a little louder, guessing the place was fairly noisy. No response again. I called even louder, far above the noise of the crowd. Nothing.

I was beginning to get scared. Had I lost the ability to hear her again? This time, not giving a shit about the people around me, I almost yelled her name. "MAAHI!"

The silence that followed was deafening, louder than the voices of all the people yelling around me. My heart in a tizzy, I took out my phone and rushed back towards the entrance. I had to let ma'am know this. Just when I was about to tap the call button on the screen after tapping in Ma'am's number, I heard the voice for which I was about to lose my mind: "Veeru, where are you going?"

"Maahi!" I yelled back at the voice which seemed to come from where a young man in a business suit and a family of three were standing separated by a few feet.

The family looked up. The young man frowned at me. Ignoring them, I called again: "Maahi!"

"I am here, Veeru." The voice now came from somewhere right next to my ear.

The young man was looking around in confusion. While it was the adults in the family who were now frowning at me, their tween daughter watching me with amused interest.

I turned sideways to face the mass of nothingness with a voice who was Maahi for me. The tween girl was about to get more entertainment looking at a man talking to thin air.

"Can you hear me?"

"Yes, I can. Why?"

"Where were you?" I asked, trying to make my voice as calm as possible.

There was silence for a few seconds. Then Maahi said: "I… I took time to say goodbye to ma'am."

"Goodbye to ma'am?"

"Yes, a last goodbye… maybe. I may never see her again."

Oh shit yes! I had forgotten that aspect of our parting. *I may never see her again.* My anger vanished. I suddenly remembered I was gazing through thin air at the being of a person who was a guest on earth – if I fulfilled my promise – for just a few more days. Who was with *me* for just a few more days. And then there would be a last goodbye with me as well. *Goodbye, I will never see you again*, she would say, and…

"Veeru!"

Her voice broke my dreamy thoughts, "What!"

"I have called you twice now! Where are you? What happened?"

"Oh, sorry," I said. "It's just that I thought I had lost the ability to hear you… again."

"Why? You can hear me quite fine…" Her voice showed surprise. "Except when you just went into a daydream."

"No… not now… I mean before this," I said. "When you were not here. I was calling for you and you were not responding. I mean… Of course you weren't there but… Just that I thought that the whole non-hearing thing was happening again and… Actually, I got shit scared. That's why I was running. To catch ma'am and tell her."

"Oh! I am sorry."

"It's ok."

"I will try not to do this again."

I smiled. "What? Last goodbyes?"

There was silence again for a while. Then she said: "No, that I have to. I have at least one more left."

Was she talking about me? I sighed. No, I guess not.

I turned around to go back to the check-in counter; we were already pretty late. That's when I saw the young man in the suit and the family, all four of them, staring at me wide-eyed. My last few minutes' performance had obviously been watched with a fair amount of interest.

I sighed. Yes, I am crazy dear friends, I am. Not only because I talk to the air, but also when you wish for a last goodbye from a ghost and then feel sad when they don't remember you… you are crazy.

MAAHI:

I have frightened him. While I was at the gate not wanting to leave ma'am, he tried talking to me, didn't get any answer and thought that he had, once again, lost the ability to hear me.

I don't tell him the truth, why I took my time. I don't want to tell him I am scared to leave ma'am. I tell him I was late because of a last goodbye we were having.

I can see he got really scared by my absence. Poor guy! I have put him through so much trouble. I promise him I will not do this again. He nods, his anxious face calming down.

We walk away as people around us stare at us or rather, stare at him, astonished. A young man in a suit with folded newspaper in hands, a pair of stylish students in jeans and colourful t-shirts, an adult couple with a pretty child.

The child, ten-eleven years old, asks her parents excitedly, "Who was he talking to?" And her parents tell her not to pay attention; some people are just crazy.

I look at Veeru. He is walking away unconcerned, but I am sure he must have heard them too. I feel angry. *He is not crazy, he is just trying hard to help me,* I want to yell at the set of oh-I-am-so-very-sane people. *He bloody cares for me.*

Yes, I realize suddenly, he cares for me, really cares about what happens to me. His face, while he was rushing back – it was so anxious, almost terrified. I realize I am not the only one frightened on this trip, I am not alone. We are both frightened, equally frightened; I for myself, he for me. I am not alone.

So that's why he came, I guess. Not for the money, but because he is concerned about me.

Suddenly, I don't feel so frightened anymore; someone else is frightened for me. I rush forward to be with him, walk beside him.

VEERU:

"Hey!" I heard her voice. She was walking right behind me as I walked to the security check.

I hesitated to reply; there was a married couple walking abreast of me on the right. With the better half of the couple walking on my side, a 'Hey!' back could be misinterpreted. The husband was a hurly burly chap, big enough to turn even me into a ghost if it took his fancy.

"It's ok. You don't have to respond," the voice said chuckling. "I don't want you to get bashed up black and blue right at the beginning of our trip."

Hmm… Maahi was reading my mind again. I glanced towards her and nodded slightly. Someone was having fun. Good.

"Have you ever teased a married woman?" was her next question.

Ya right! Wasn't that the only thing left in the world for me to do? Of course, after taking a ghost to Goa in search for her unknown lover.

"Have you ever got your ass kicked for eve-teasing?"

I frowned. What was this sudden preoccupation with eve-teasing? And how come the sudden chirpiness in the mood?

"It's ok," she went on. "You can confess to me. I won't tell anyone. Actually, it's better. I am a ghost; I *can't* tell anyone."

And so on and on it went, my pretty ghost's monologue. After teasing me about eve-teasing, she speculated on the reasons why the burly, bald husband could have lost his hair and laid the chief blame on his wife's doorstep; then analysed the frown on a security guard's face and was ready to bet it had something to do with his mother-in-law and pressed me some five times to confirm (I actually did; it turned out he had a stomach-ache); further on, mused on the grave injustice of allowing men inside the plane and yet banning deodorants from it (reminding me of the fact that I hadn't taken a bath today); and lastly, while I was standing in front of the metal detector for the check, wondered if as a ghost she was still a citizen of India, and so was it constitutionally ok for her to bypass the check and why didn't our founding fathers make their position clearer on the tangled issue of citizenship for departed beings still stuck in earthly prisons. While I didn't reply, I couldn't help smiling at her musings (except for the one about the deodorant!).

Once out of the security check and having found that our flight was late by around forty minutes, I went around and discovered a place to stand in the lounge area – I made sure it was out of sight of most people and out of hearing of all. Then I pretended to admire a painting of a beautiful Rajasthani villager winnowing rice as her daughter looked on and Maahi continued her musings about the outlook of our founding fathers on ghosts.

"Do you think Gandhi believed in ghosts?"

"I have no clue."

"I think I read somewhere he did when he was a kid. He thought they lived in the dark and would catch him and eat him." She sighed.

I glanced at her. "Don't be disheartened. All kids think similarly. Even the one who grows up to be the father of the nation."

"I am not disheartened. Who knows Gandhi was right even as a kid. I may still eat you."

"You'll eat me?"

"Uh… maybe…" she paused. "Not right now anyway. It's not dark yet." She paused again. "On second thoughts… actually no. You are too skinny, and too fair, and don't look tasty enough. I would rather eat chocolate. *Dark* chocolate. I am a creature of the *dark*."

"Thanks for the compliment!"

"Which one? Too skinny or too fair or worse than chocolate?"

"All of them."

"Always a pleasure. Do you think Nehru believed in ghosts?"

"I have no clue," I repeated.

"Ambedkar?"

"No clue again!"

"Patel?"

I glanced at her again. "Why this sudden fascination with freedom fighters?"

"Not only freedom fighters. They wrote the constitution too. And I think it's unfair towards—"

"Ghosts?"

"Yes! They never even so much as *mentioned* us! What about our ghostly rights? Are we equal to, like… you guys? And what if there is an election while I am still stuck on earth? Shouldn't I get a vote? I mean I am not yet quite… dead."

"You are not?"

"No! Isn't it obvious? My soul still lives on, even though I have shuffled off the mortal coil. Come to the realm of not-to-be. Seeking the oblivion…"

"What?"

"What what? What did you not understand? Mortal coil? That means… the ups and downs of my life. I mean my soul still lives on even if my life is over."

"And your soul wants equality?"

"Of course!"

"And the right to vote?"

"You bet!"

"And chocolate."

"Oh yes! That too. Dark chocolate. My daaark soul wants daaark creamy chocolate."

"Anything else?"

"Oh, much more. The list is long." She paused. "Anyway, leave that. Does that painting beat the Mona Lisa?"

"Why?"

"Don't you think you have looked at that painting for like… really long?"

"Yes. I am fascinated by it."

"See! I so *knew* you were into married women!"

"Ha ha ha… very funny!" I paused to consider. Should I? Then I decided to go ahead. "Ok, Maahi… tell me one thing?"

"Huh?"

"I have a question in mind."

"You seem to be serious…" she paused. "Hmm… is that a difficult question you are going to ask?"

I didn't know what to say. Was it? Yes, maybe. "Maybe."

"Thought so. Your voice said as much."

She sighed. "Has that question got something to do with like… the names of Patel and Nehru and all?"

I nodded, "Sort of."

"I knew," she said, knowing as usual. "Okay… shoot."

She puzzled me. What had transformed her all of a sudden from a sad to a totally saucy ghost? I asked my question anyway: "If you remember uh… things like names of freedom fighters, our constitution, right to vote, dark creamy chocolate and all, then uh… why can't you remember who you are? I mean it looks like you know everything but those few—"

"Yes, I know," she said, "Strange isn't it?"

Strange that she remembered everything. Almost everything, except for her identity – who she was and her relationships, her family and friends.. She even remembered that she loved dark chocolate. That she had come to this airport many times. And that she had never voted. Everything but…

Strange. She paused. "Any idea why?"

I shook my head.

She sighed. "Just my luck. I asked ma'am too and even she didn't know."

My question, it seemed from her voice, had left her a little down. So to change the topic, and therefore hopefully her mood, I asked her in a scandalized tone: "By the way, you never voted? Really?"

"No."

"I can't believe—"

"Before you wax on more about your disbelief," she reminded me, "remember I was probably no more than twenty-five when I kicked the bucket."

And so, she told me, I should also remember that since it was 2013, she could have voted in just one general election which she didn't. Which was not an unpardonable crime.

"Still," I shrugged. "Someone, if I rightly recall, was seconds ago grumbling about not having the right to vote!"

"Shame on you!" My pretty ghost dished me a tangent.

"Shame on me? Where did that come from?"

"I am a damsel in distress! You should help me… poor me. Instead you are taking my case!"

Ya right! "A damsel in distress who not long ago threatened to *eat* me, remember?"

"That's not fair," she replied in an injured tone. "Don't hold that against me. I didn't threaten to eat you. I just temporarily considered you as an option and dropped you in favour of dark chocolate."

"Oh thanks! Never been more flattered!"

She giggled. "I know. I am good at it. Dark chocolate…" She paused. "That reminds me… Shouldn't I get some favour in return for not eating you?"

"Favour… Like what?"

"Like the option of at least looking at chocolates even if the time for me having them is past? We have time to *look* at least… don't we? Till the time for boarding and taking off comes."

And so just in a few words, she made me glimpse the pain that lay behind all the attempts at humour. She wasn't happy, but she was pretending to be happy. Why? I mean, was it for… me?

Suddenly, I wanted to look at her face. I wanted to look into her eyes, to know what she really felt. I wanted to go beyond the wall of that pepped up voice, the mask of those happy, light words. It was perhaps impossible, but I wished I could.

And I wanted to touch her. Hold her and comfort her. Tell her that I understand her, that she need not pretend with me. That I will be there for her, whether she was happy or sad. She need not pretend.

"Where are you lost?" It was her happy voice again. "I am dying to see dark chocolates! We don't have time. And here you are lost again!"

And tell her that I'll feed her… dark chocolate?

The rest of the time till the time the final call came, we looked at, discussed and joked about chocolates.

MAAHI:

After I let go of my fear because I know Veeru fears for me, cares for me, I also vow to let go of self-pity. Walking ahead of me, he shrugs off the unkindly comments of people as if they were nothing. He is doing that for me, a stranger. I decide I can't burden him with self-pity on top of that.

That moment, the pain in me lessens. Though it still feels as if a wild animal was clawing my insides, the claws feel less sharp. As if the decision to stop feeling sorry for myself, to be stronger, has suddenly blunted their sharpness.

I may still be in pain, but why should that stop me from laughing, I ask. Why should that stop me from making Veeru laugh? He bears my burden for no reason except that I need his help. Then why shouldn't I try to lessen it with my laughter, my jokes, instead of making it heavier with the boulders of self-pity.

I resolve I will not feel sorry for myself. I will *not*. I will make a lot of jokes instead; become a joker in my last few days. I will go into the oblivion laughing, even if not happily.

"Why do you like dark chocolate so much?" he asks softly turning over a Hershey's bar. Our backs are turned towards the rest of the shop. We are window shopping as we wait for the final call.

I take a few seconds to think. Then I answer in a gloomy tone: "Because dark chocolate is so… so *bitter*. I guess I liked its bitterness. Tasted the way I feel."

I get a sharp glance, and he gazes in my direction for some time trying to figure out what happened. Finally, he decides I am serious. "I am sorr—" he begins, looking a lot like an earnest but confused and unhappy schoolboy.

"Don't look so sad," I tell him giggling. "I am just pulling your leg. The real reason is different."

Then I explain dark chocolate is not only bitter, it's healthy too. Healthier than white or milk chocolate. I guess that's why I preferred it.

He grins, "So you are a health freak… is it?"

"No, I am not a health freak," I say reminding him of my ghostly status. "I *was* a health freak."

He laughs at my correction. "Ok, miss grammar! Got it. You *were* a health freak." He pauses. "Were you?"

"Maybe. Asmi ma'am told me I have a figure worth envying."

"Or *had* a figure worth envying?" He bites his lip.

"Haa haa… touché. I—"

"You know something?" he interrupts. His eyebrows are up and his eyes are twinkling. "I think you are yourself a little like dark chocolate."

"Me? Why?"

"Yes, you are. Like a sweet dark chocolate." He chuckles. "Miss Dark Chocolaty. A little bitter, but much more sweet."

I giggle at the name. "Dark Chocolaty? Oh yes! The dark bitterness in my soul… " I say giving it back. "But don't forget, unlike dark chocolate, I am *not* good for your health. I can eat you."

"But I thought you preferred dark chocolate over me?" He puts up a mock frown.

I giggle some more. "Don't be so sure," I tell him. "With your smile and your compliments, you are growing on me." I run my tongue over my lips and make a smacking sound. "You are in great danger of being gobbled up."

He grins, but says nothing.

"You are grinning. But really… what if I grow more bitter than sweet before the trip ends? You could be in mortal danger."

He grins wider. "Maybe. But I'll take my chance."

Take my chance? That reminds me of something. I let out a sigh. *I wish I had a chance too*, I am tempted to say.

Then I remember my vow; no more self-pity. And I don't.

VEERU:

To board, we waited till the time we were almost sure that we were the last two souls boarding the plane. At the check-in counter, I had coaxed Maahi's ticket out of the ticketing executive by fibbing with a glowing smile that Maahi was my friend about to turn-up any moment. But now that she was sure to be labelled a no-show after being absent at the departure gate, we wanted to make sure that the time between that happening and the plane taking-off was so little that the airlines would have no chance of giving her seat to anyone else.

I wondered, of course, if Maahi really needed a seat. Not aloud; that would have been the height of incivility. But in my mind… yes.

I mean what did she feel when she sat somewhere?

Like us, did she feel the solidness of the seat beneath… or what? How did she stay on the seat instead of just sinking through it? She was a ghost right – just a soul, a spirit. And weren't spirits supposed to be like made of thin air or energy or something?

Now I hadn't felt her flying through the air or anything; from what I had guessed when she talked to me, she had always taken the normal walking-on-the-ground route. But then I had never really seen her. With the help of her voice, I had just estimated where she was at different times. I could be wrong.

I had wanted to ask her those questions once or twice – the ones about the typical characteristics of ghosts I had read about in books or seen in movies. Could she really glide through the air like they showed in the movies? Could she walk through solid walls? Could she make the electrical equipment malfunction and also make the air cold? Could she perform the epitome of all ghostly powers: teleportation?

Umm... as for making the air cold, she definitely didn't. I had never felt any change in temperature while she sat or walked beside me. But you never know; maybe she was just being nice to me.

The airline executive at the departure gate number 18, Vasavi, was also nice to me – when I fibbed to her that my travelling companion was not with me because she had suddenly taken ill and gone back and since I too wasn't feeling great, could Vasavi make sure that there was no one sitting next or even next to next to me?

With a big smile Vasavi told me that she was sorry, but that wasn't possible; all the seats had already been allocated. My friend wasn't coming, so the seat next to me would certainly be empty; but not the seat next to that as it was already allocated. However, if I wanted, she will inform the cabin crew about me not feeling well if I could also tell her what was responsible for my lack of wellness – wrong food or viral fever or... what? Should she?

To which I said hastily, "No, that won't be necessary," and walked through the gate hoping Maahi was with me. Moments later, I heard her sweet, familiar voice as I descended to catch the bus that would take us to the plane. I was relieved; she had followed me.

"So why aren't you feeling well... *sir*?" she asked me with a chuckle. "Is it because of the annoying ghost behind you?"

That's when my phone buzzed.

"Shut up, Miss Chocolaty!" I told Maahi in a loud whisper grinning as I took my phone out.

I shouldn't have done that! At the words, the person going down ahead of me – a lady in her mid-thirties in a crisp and starched maroon sari – turned sharply with a deep frown that seemed about to turn into a glare. I grimaced. I thought I had kept the volume of my '*Shut up*' low enough!

Luckily, as Maahi started laughing behind me, the glance of the wrong Miss Chocolaty fell on the phone in my hand. Understanding seemed to dawn on her face, (a totally wrong understanding of course), and her face returned to normal. She turned back, convinced I was talking on my phone to some other woman and it was to that woman I had addressed my sweet nothing.

I sighed with relief! Thank God for cell phones!

And I was enlightened; yes, this was it. This was how I could talk to Maahi even in crowded places without the risk of being thought a madman! I was so happy that I could have actually hugged the maroony lady for showing me the serendipitous solution.

I looked at the SMS Asmi ma'am had sent me before I almost got into trouble. *Have you guys boarded?*

I raised the phone to my left ear, "Maahi, I got an SMS from ma'am," I said into the phone.

"Oh cool!" Maahi said, still chuckling at my Miss-Chocolaty gaffe.

"She is asking if we have boarded."

"Write back to her saying I am already missing her."

I rolled my eyes. Girls it seemed didn't leave their sentimental selves behind even after they became ghosts.

So I wrote back to ma'am: *No, not boarded. But we r about 2 get in the ferry bus. And Maahi says she's already missing u.*

Ma'am's reply came after we had got on the bus and it had just started moving: *Tell Maahi I am missing her too.*

And of course girls didn't change after they became old professors of Molecular Biophysics either!

I wrote back: *Sure ma'am. Will tell her.*"

How is Maahi doing? Ma'am replied soon.

Yelling in my ear, what are u writing, I replied. Maahi had yelled that in my ears just a second back. *So I guess pretty gud.*

How are you *doing? :-)* came Ma'am's reply with a smiley.

Am being yelled in my ear by an inquisitive ghost, so guess I am doing pretty gud 2, I wrote.

"I am yelling in your ears?" That was Maahi again. "If only I had a real body dude!" she threatened me in a deep voice as she read the messages over my shoulder. By that time, the bus had stopped next to the plane and we happened to be the last two to get off the vehicle.

Yes, ghosts are quite inquisitive, Ma'am wrote as we climbed the stairs that would take us into the plane. *They miss their lives just gone by… that's why. They want to know about everything.*

I had just experienced that, *Tell me about it!* I wrote. *Maahi even wants to know about my eve-teasing preferences. Now we know what she is missing in her life!*

Just before we entered the plane, I couldn't resist turning to Maahi, "Was that why you asked me about married women?" I asked raising the phone to my ear. "God!" I paused significantly in front of the cabin crew. "Don't tell me you… you really teased married women?"

I don't know how Maahi reacted to that. But the welcoming members of the cabin crew, both females, maybe married too, stared at me with wide eyes while I passed them as if talking on the phone. Proud of my comeback, I chuckled and strolled on after giving them a radiant smile.

If I knew what lay ahead of me in the seats, I wouldn't have done that.

MAAHI:

I look at Veeru as he glibly lies to the airline's executive Vasavi to explain my apparent absence; and then lies some more and pretends to be unwell to try and get the seat next to us empty. He fails, but I can't help but smile at his straight-faced bluffs.

Did I really need a ticket? I somehow know that Veeru wonders about that among other things – things like whether I can fly through air or walk through walls. I wonder because I don't know myself yet; I haven't checked out my ghostly characteristics yet.

To tell the truth, I am afraid to check out. It's easier being a ghost than accepting being one.

I know that I am more like a human mind than anything else; like a mind, I can be wherever I want to be *if* I know where exactly I want to be. I mean when coming with Asmi ma'am to the airport in the morning – my first time out of ma'am's home since I became a ghost – there was this moment in the car when I couldn't read a billboard advertisement with a pretty child in it; and I wished I was there right next to it so I could read it.

And you know what? The next moment, I was actually there! Right next to the advertisement staring into the eyes of the child painted half as big as my face. Almost a hundred feet above the ground!

I was scared out of my wits; and more than the fact that I was hanging a hundred feet in the air, I was scared that I was alone and lost. Where was the car? Where was ma'am?

I looked down at the flyover on which I was passing by in a red hatchback not a moment ago, and I saw the car descending down the slope of the flyover. Soon it would get lost among the crowd of cars rushing up the road and merge in with the higher traffic at the signal not far ahead. Panic gripped my throat; I didn't know what to do.

And then thankfully, I saw the hatchback slowing down and stopping by the side of the road once it had reached the highway. A tiny looking ma'am got out of the car and started searching for me. But though she was looking all around herself, she was just looking at her eye level; she wasn't looking up.

Look up! I wished I could yell in her ear. *I am up here. Here up at the billboard.*

And the next moment, I was actually standing next to her, my mouth close to her ear, about to yell.

After we got back into the car and were back on course to the airport, ma'am explained to me what had happened. We ghosts were like human minds, she said; and so I had the ability to teleport myself to a place of choice, meaning I would immediately be at that place provided I could visualize it and wanted to be there. So I should remember this fact and teleport only deliberately if required, and then with some amount of caution. And even if I managed to teleport myself accidentally to someplace undesirable, I shouldn't panic and teleport myself back to wherever I was.

So, did I need the air ticket to Goa when I could teleport myself? I had asked ma'am not to waste money on one; even if I wasn't teleporting myself and going with Veeru in the good old-fashioned aerial way, I didn't need a *paid-for* seat. I was sure that in the early morning flight there would be at least one seat that was empty, especially since it was offseason in Goa, and I would take that. Or even if I couldn't find a proper seat, I could grab a place anywhere – maybe even one right next to the pilot on the cockpit. I am sure the airlines wouldn't mind a ticketless person if she happened to be a ghost.

But ma'am wouldn't hear of it. She said in her determined voice that ghost or not, I was a soul, as good as any person. And every soul above the age of two years on a plane required a proper seat and a proper ticket, so I must have a ticket.

I am already missing that determined voice; I am missing ma'am. My heart constricts when I remember I may never see her again, hear that voice face to face again. So when ma'am messages Veeru to ask if we have boarded the plane yet, I ask him to message her back that I am missing her. He rolls his eyes but does that.

Then we get back to teasing each other. He complains to ma'am that I am an inquisitive ghost yelling into his ears; and I threaten him with bodily harm if only I had a body. Our conversation goes on to ghosts inquisitive about eve-teasing married women, a dispute that scandalizes the two pretty women welcoming us inside the plane. Feeling deliciously evil, I hope they are married.

I don't know things are about to get more interesting.

VEERU:

Our seats were in row eighteen – number A and B. Despite my lying, I wasn't able to get an empty seat next to us. So walking through the aisle when we reached close to our seats, I saw that seat number C was occupied by a pretty girl about my age. Maahi obviously noticed her at the same time because immediately, I heard a wolf-whistle behind me followed by a slurp and a lecherous comment,

"Ooh... What a hot chick!"

I ignored the comment, put on a polite smile, walked up to the pretty girl and requested her to give way.

"Oh sure!" she said with a smile and got up. Meanwhile Maahi was hissing like a maniac behind me.

"Take the middle seat, dude! Take the middle seat!"

Ignoring her again, I moved forward to take the window seat A. Just as I was about to sit down, I heard Maahi's voice come from right below me.

"Take the middle seat!" it ordered like some Nawab of Lucknow. She had somehow moved ahead of me and had grabbed the window seat!

I flinched back, drawing a surprised look from the other girl. What could I say to her?

"Uh... I think I saw a spider," I said lamely. The girl nodded.

"Liar!" My nawabi friend perched comfortably on *my* seat observed. "No one would believe you were afraid of spiders."

She was right! And I suddenly realized what I had ended up meaning because of my unprepared lie – a quite well-built guy of twenty-five was afraid of spiders!

My male ego, having taken a hit, needed some bandaging. Hastily, I lied to the pretty girl again.

"Not that I mind spiders, but I was surprised to find a big one here."

The girl, her lips starting to curl just a little, nodded graciously but didn't say anything.

"Whaaat!" Maahi hollered. "Do you realize you just made things worse?"

A cute guy fearing spiders was excusable, maybe even cuter. A guy covering up fearing spiders was not!

I sighed. As if things could get worse. With a pretty ghost lecturing me and a pretty girl thinking I was a dumbass.

"Are you going to sit down?" the girl asked.

I was in a dilemma. "Uh…"

"You want to sit on my lap?" Maahi asked with a giggle.

That offer made the choice clear.

"I don't mind," Maahi went on, "but I will need a mid-air lap dance as payment."

Her giggles wouldn't stop as she completed the sentence.

I grimaced! Not having a choice, I sat down on the middle seat and gave the girl on my right a polite smile. She returned the smile even more politely.

"You don't want to sit on my lap?" the leg-pulling continued.

No! But I do want to strangle your ghostly neck… Miss Maahi whatever!

The worse thing was I couldn't even reply to those expert comments for the next one hour till we landed in Goa. The cabin crew would give the command to switch off the cell phones soon, so even the trick with the phone couldn't be tried.

"You know the chick's gonna think you made up the spider excuse to sit next to her," was Maahi's next observation.

As if I didn't know that!

I gave a quick sideways glance at the said 'chick'. She was fiddling with an i-Pod. I wished I had an i-Pod too.

"You are wishing for an i-Pod?"

I turned my head towards the empty window seat. How could she so clearly read my thoughts? When I couldn't even see her?

"I don't know how I can read your thoughts but—"

"Maahi!" I couldn't help exclaiming, I was so annoyed. I mean what could I do? She just kept answering to my *thoughts*!

The girl on the right jerked up from her i-Pod and looked at me in confusion. "Yes? You said something?"

I was caught again. I told her another lie. "No… I… I thought *you* said something."

She frowned. "Did I? No, I didn't."

I *know* that. "Oh… ok."

I wanted to glare at Maahi for putting me in this absurd position; and I couldn't. I wanted to yell at her; I couldn't either. All I could do was sit there and feel like an utter ass.

"I thought of a way we can talk," Maahi went on happily. "Take out your laptop once the plane takes off. Then I can talk, you just type. That way—"

And can you not answer my thoughts till then?

"And I will not answer your thoughts till then."

Aaaaaaaah… I gave up.

MAAHI:

The girl on the aisle seat is pretty, quite pretty; and she arouses in me this overwhelming desire to play the matchmaker. I whistle the moment I see her. Surprisingly, I find I am a natural. I follow up the whistle with a cheap comment and see my friend, philosopher and guide… no, just friend and guide, (I don't think Veeru will appreciate being called a philosopher), shaking his head. Yup… I am doubtful he would have dreamt in a million years that someday he would have to travel with an eve-teasing ghost.

Fortunately for him, my eve-teasing is harmless. No girl would ever come to know of my unearthly vulgar comments or of my ghastly lecherous smiles.

After I have bamboozled my friend and guide into sitting next to the aisle-seat girl (fear of lap dancing playing important role in the act of persuasion), I tell him to get his laptop out once the plane takes off. That way we can talk to each other: he can type, I can speak. He nods, already exasperated by my ability to read his thoughts.

I don't know how I do that. I can't explain to him that I am not exactly *reading* his thoughts; I mean that's a wrong way to put it. Rather the moment I look at him, his thoughts sometimes jump into my mind and skip through it. As if I am not reading them; as if the thoughts are simply swinging into my head, like naughty, unruly monkeys swinging from one branch to another. I guess I won't be able to stop them even if I want to.

And I guess I don't want to either.

VEERU:

"Talk to her!" she hissed from my left.

I ignored her again. This was the fourth time Maahi had said those words and her tone was getting more and more insistent each time.

"Why can't you talk to her? Are you that shy?"

I pursed my lips and stared at the seat in front firmly.

"Or are you gay?"

That pushed me over the line. I got out my laptop and started typing.

```
Yes, I am gay. Makes you happy?
```

"Oh come on. I saw you glance at her boobs as you crossed her. Don't lie."

I did no such thing!

"Did too… but I don't blame you. They are worth glancing at."

Can we talk of something else beside her boobs?

"No, I am an eve-teaser. I am verrry interested in her boobs. Especially if she is married."

Ya, right!

And then from the corner of my eyes, I saw the girl in question looking at my laptop. Shit! Had she read what I had just typed? I hoped she hadn't. I quickly deleted the lines about her boobs and pulled the laptop closer and slowly turned it sideways as if adjusting for more comfort.

I heard Maahi giggling. "Did she read it?"

Yes… I think so! Thanks!

A giggle again, "Don't worry. She will be happy you like her boobs. She totally digs you."

Why are you fixated on her boobs?

More giggles, "Because they are fantastic. They look so soft and round and plump and jui—"

I elbowed furiously where Maahi should have been.

"Don't hit me! Okay… I'll stop. I like her eyes too by the way. They are filled with admiration."

Admiration?

"Yes, admiration. For you, my friend. Just for you. Dripping with admiration… and desire. Look… look."

Haa haa haa. Good joke.

"I am serious! She is dying for you to talk to her."

For a guy afraid of imaginary spiders?

"Why not? Maybe she thinks guys making up stories about spiders to sit next to her are sexy."

That's creepy, not sexy!

"How do you know? Are you a girl? We girls have varied tastes."

Are you done?

"No, I am not. Why don't you talk to her and find out for yourself what she finds sexy and what not?"

I am going to sleep.

I pulled down the monitor of my laptop, tilted my seat, leaned back, and closed my eyes.

Many minutes passed by before Maahi spoke again. "What if this plane crashes today?" It was almost a whisper.

Startled, I opened my eyes and sat up slowly.

"Suddenly, everything comes to an end. I don't know how the crash I was in happened…" she went on almost dreamily.

"I don't remember. But it must have been sudden." Her voice, seeming to be focused far far away, was like a pair of unseeing eyes.

"I may have been sitting like you, looking forward to things to come. Maybe beautiful things. And then…" She paused.

I kept silent.

"We think we have all the time in the world, isn't it? But sometimes we don't. Things go wrong suddenly. Sometimes…"

She stopped abruptly. "I am sorry. I don't know what came over me."

"It's ok," I typed. "You want me to talk to her?" I wanted to distract her from painful thoughts.

"Yes. You would look nice together. Time… don't let it go by like this… carelessly. We should clutch at the moments we have. Before eternity comes, before we drown in eternity. I feel… you and her… if… It would make sense before I go away."

She sounded so forlorn. I didn't know what to say. I wanted to touch her. But there was no hand of hers next to me to hold. I wish —

"You want to hold her hand?" Maahi piped up cutting into my thoughts. "I like that spirit!"

Excitement had returned into her voice. I smiled.

She had read my mind again. But this time, she had misunderstood it.

MAAHI:

I don't know what came over me. I am sitting there, watching Veeru pretending to sleep, watching the girl giving him covert glances, obviously wishing him to notice her and talk to her, when suddenly I am furious. I want to give Veeru a resounding slap. 'Wake up, you idiot!' I want to yell at him. Time is going by. I feel like an extremely poor and hungry girl watching rich people waste food blissfully. I want to grab Veeru's hair and shake him furiously till he is blue. Wake up! One day you will be poor too. Damn rich people. I feel like a time communist.

And then, as suddenly as it had come, the anger evaporates. What remains is an intense sense of loneliness, of separation, of being different. They are different, they are rich. Why should they care? They have time.

It's me who is poor… and afraid. For the first time, I am scared of the oblivion, of eternity. I am very scared. How would it feel like? Ma'am had said that the question itself was meaningless; there was no 'I', no consciousness to feel anything. It was just… nothing. An oblivion.

I was happy then, happy to hear that. It was comforting as a concept, especially when the pain inside me kept getting more and more difficult to bear every day. I was tired. I just wanted to find my love and escape the intense pain. So I welcomed the oblivion and was looking forward to the day when I would dissolve into nothingness. I would be free.

But now as I look at a sleeping Veeru and the nameless girl, I am not so sure if I want the oblivion that much. I am not sure if I want to be free. I want to find... *him*... but I don't want to leave. What is worse? This pain... or... or to feel nothing.

I don't want the nothingness. I am scared of it. It sounds so terribly lonely out there. An eternal loneliness.

I look at Veeru, at his smooth, wide forehead mottled by a few stray strands, at his eyes that will be dark brown when he opens them, at his slightly flat nose, at his wide, thin lips, at his light blue shirt through which I get a peek of his white vest, at the gentle undulations of his breast conveying life and warmth. He looks very cute sleeping that way. No wonder the other girl keeps sneaking glances at him.

I run my fingers slowly through the strands falling on his forehead, fingers that of course he would never feel. I am a ghost, and poorer than a church mouse where time is concerned – seven more days to go on earth if I am lucky and we do find *him*. A ghost with almost no time left to her account. Time that passes with every beat of his heart.

He doesn't know how precious every one of those beats is. He must know. He must get up. Talk to the girl. I must tell him.

I tell him. But instead of getting my urgency and starting to talk to the girl that very minute, he gazes at me with kind eyes.

I feel the anger in me rising again. I want to slap him again. Why can't he just turn towards her and talk? I don't want his kindness. It makes me angry.

You want me to talk to her? he types.

Yes, that's what I want. Before going, I want to see him fall in love; I want to see a blooming love affair. I don't know why I want that, but I know I want that. Desperately. It would make everything else somehow more sensible, bearable. I want him to find his love as much as I want to find mine. And when you have just seven days to fall in love, who better than the first pretty girl you look at!

I guess I am acting very selfishly, but I have a hunch the nameless girl will make for a good girlfriend. Oh hell! I don't know. I just hope so. But he will never know unless he talks to her, will he?

Talk to her dude!

That's when another of his thoughts skips through my mind. He wants to comfort me... and he wants to hold my hand. My hand! What?

No, I must have got it wrong. He must have wanted to hold *her* hand. They are beautiful too. Nice, long delicate fingers. They would be good hands to hold. But how will he *ever* unless he starts talking to her?

At last, he starts talking to her as the cabin crew wheels in the refreshments. I breathe a ghostly sigh of relief. Her name is Ghazal. What a beautiful name! I have surely never come across anyone of that name before. I mean I am as sure as a ghost can be.

"Do you know any ghazals?" I whisper with a giggle in Veeru's ears as he tells Ghazal his name.

He smiles, trying not to laugh. She is smiling too, happy that he is talking to her. They are both smiling. Such a cute couple, I am sure they will be happy. I feel quite proud of myself. The fastest Emma the world may have ever seen.

I start singing softly. *Aaj jaane ki zidd na karo, yunhi pehlu mein baithe raho*. Don't insist on going today. Keep sitting by my side like this. It's a beautiful ghazal.

VEERU:

Her name was Ghazal. She was originally from Kanpur, now working in Bangalore in a PR firm, and she was flying to Goa to join a group of colleagues from her office. And I had no idea why I was talking to her except that for some inconceivable reason Maahi thought she was the Juliet to my Romeo self. I mean the way Maahi was going on, it would have seemed certain to anyone eavesdropping that me and my newly anointed Juliet were fated to die in each other's arms when the plane crashed not minutes later. All that remained for us was to proclaim our undying love for each other as Maahi sung her favourite ghazals in my ear before we all kicked the bucket (except for her, of course, since she had *already* kicked the bucket).

The only reason I was going through this was Maahi. If this pantomime comforted her, so be it. And she sang sweetly enough to make up for it. Suited to her ghostly self, her voice had a haunting, far-away feel to it. As if a lady in white was singing to herself walking through a quiet forest.

Aaj jaane ki zidd na karo.

Don't be adamant on going today.

If anyone, the person who the song should have been sung to was Maahi herself – the one going away, soon, if not today.

Instead she was singing it for me and Ghazal, two strangers in a plane, having nothing to do with each other.

My idea? *Pal do pal ka saath hamara* would have perhaps suited us better.

Despite several of Maahi's melodious entreaties, which Ghazal had no idea of, my temporary Juliet blissfully went away to join her colleagues after we landed in Goa about a quarter of an hour later. We exchanged numbers on my request before we parted at the airport; I knew Maahi – having reminded me thrice to do so – would have my happiness if I didn't.

Though I had no intentions of calling Ghazal, I went through the motions; I had to do whatever made the invisible girl standing behind me happy. And she did sound happy.

Hopefully, she would forget all this Ghazal nonsense once we started the search for her identity and for the unknown man she loved, the man who she had named Hrithik. I had a hunch the search was soon going to turn frantic; we were already racing against time, and I was afraid the race was going to become tougher and tougher.

After letting Asmi ma'am know that we had reached safely, we went into the city and I found a room in a hotel where I had stayed the last time I had come: a hotel Residency Annexe near the Calangute beach. I had planned on taking two rooms, but I dropped the plan when Maahi protested against this wasteful expenditure (her words). Since being a ghost she neither needed a bathroom nor a bed, she said there was no reason why we should take a second room just for her and throw away precious money.

"You don't need a bed?" I asked her once we were inside our room. "Why… you don't sleep?"

"No."

"Then what do you do at night?"

She said she just wandered around. For the past six days, it had been mostly in Asmi ma'am's garden.

"Just wander around?"

"Yes."

I opened my mouth to say something, then closed it.

Useless. She had already read my mind.

"Yes… it's lonely," she said answering my thought. "I know. But… what choice do I have?"

Yes, what choice did she have? "Maybe… maybe you can close your eyes and lie down?"

She sighed. "You know… you sometimes think just like me. I actually tried that. Many times. It didn't help. I guess sleep is not for wandering souls like me. I will sleep only when I have found the oblivion. And then… I won't wake up."

"Don't talk like that!"

"What? That I won't wake up? You know it's true. Death and taxes… no escaping them."

I could almost picture her grinning at her twinge of humour. I felt a stab of pain in my heart.

"You are really looking forward to it, aren't you? To the oblivion?"

"Yes, a little sleep would be good. I am a little tired."

"A little sleep?"

She ignored my question. "Have you called Ghazal?"

"Ghazal? Why?"

"Check whether she found her friends and got to her hotel safely."

I smiled. The dead was worrying whether the living had reached its destination safely. I didn't tell Maahi I much doubted whether a few days later Ghazal would remember I even existed. I had extensive experience with the type: quick to make friends, quick to fall in 'love', quick to break hearts, quick to forget.

"Will call her later. Now we have to hurry."

"Where are we going?" Maahi asked.

"To the transport department. They should have a record of all the accidents."

The transport department headquarters was located in West Panaji in a building called Junta House situated close to the mouth of the river Mandovi. It was a ride of about thirty minutes on the bike I had hired from the hotel. We found our way in, and after a short delay, we were directed to a room that accommodated about fifteen people working behind their desks. The room looked fairly congested and we were wondering who to go to when a middle-aged lady with oval frames and hennaed hair sitting on our left beckoned me. I obediently ambled to her desk and told her what I wanted.

She nodded at my story. "And she was your…?" She paused significantly.

"A second cousin," I lied. Then I told her a quick but detailed rigmarole I had already crafted with Maahi's help that involved star-crossed lovers from Bihar, unwilling hard-as-nails parents, and a troubled, runaway girl who was last believed to be in Goa with her boyfriend and then had vanished after supposedly meeting with an accident. I explained the families involved didn't want a scandal, and the parents on both sides had softened considerably since their rebellious offspring had disappeared, so they were carrying out a joint private search before they went to the police. All that the families now wanted was to find their children and get them married. The story regarding Goa had reached them just one day before, and I happened to be in Goa by chance, so I had been called up by my almost crying aunt and ordered to find out more information without revealing her daughter's name.

The lady nodded seriously at my tall tale, her face showing concern and considerable interest.

"Really… what a horribly good liar you are!" Maahi piped up from behind. "Look at her face. She has no doubt you are telling the truth."

I was much tempted to turn around and tell her "I know".

"So…" the lady asked. "You don't want to tell me your cousin's name at all? It would be easier—"

"I know, ma'am. But my aunt made me promise I will not reveal Kokil's name while searching. Kokil is her pet name," I smiled sweetly.

"Kokil. Hmm… Now I got a pet name too," Maahi said giggling. "I like that."

The lady, oblivious to Maahi's words, nodded. "Shouldn't be that difficult. There would only be a few accidents involving a young girl. How old did you say your cousin was?"

"About twenty-five, ma'am."

"And you are sure the day of the accident was 21st July?"

"Almost sure, ma'am."

"Hmm… let's see. We have a record of twelve road accidents on 21st July. One of them had a girl of twenty-three in it. Serious, but not fatal. Name Sylvia D'Souza. Very much a Goan name. I am sure she can't be your Kokil? Isn't it?"

"No, ma'am."

"Another accident involved a girl of twenty-five. She died… I am sorry—" My heart leapt up. "Her name was Anusuya Chettiyar." My heart came down. "She also doesn't seem… I believe you said your cousin was from Bihar?"

"Yes, ma'am," I nodded. "No, it can't be Anusuya Chettiyar. You're sure it *is* Chettiyar?"

The lady nodded. "Yes, the records show the body was positively identified by her family." She paused. "There is one more accident with a lady who was thirty-two… Tarannum Begum. No, she can't be your Kokil either."

I nodded again. "No."

"I am sorry. There is no one who seems to…"

She paused. "You're sure the accident happened on 21st July?"

I didn't reply immediately, waiting. Maahi read my mind. "Quite sure," she said softly.

"Quite sure," I repeated.

"I am sorry then. Who told your family that your cousin was in an accident?"

"Someone from the guy's side told my uncle," I replied keeping it vague enough.

"Maybe they got wrong information about the…"

I nodded. "Possible."

Suddenly, the lady brightened up. "Or there is one more possibility. Go to the Quepem office of the Assistant Director of Transport."

"Quepem?"

She nodded. "It's in South Goa."

She said sometimes the Quepem office had records of recent accidents in South Goa that the Junta House office didn't get to know about immediately. Of course the chance that something like that would have happened was quite low since seven days had already gone by since the accident, but one never knew and there was no harm trying.

Yes, there was no harm trying. I thanked the lady profusely for her help, and came out of the office.

"To Quepem then?" I asked my invisible companion with a bright smile.

"Yes… to Quepem. You think it will help?" she asked in a small voice.

I sidestepped her question. "We keep checking until we find who you are and then find Hrithik," I said in a firm voice.

The Quepem office of the Assistant Director of Transport was a drive of an hour and a half from Junta House. By the time we reached the place, it was lunch-time. We had to wait for almost forty-five minutes while the break lasted. And then despite giving the reference of Ms Kerkar, the lady who had helped us in Junta House, it took us another two hours to meet the right person: a bearded man with sunken eyes and a lethargic, disinterested voice.

The meeting was over in less than five minutes. The man said they didn't have any records from 21st July that the Junta House people didn't already have. Then we were asked to leave; he had important work. It was all very official, almost rude. The man sounded as if there were too many runaway girls in the country meeting with accidents everyday to bother his precious head about!

F**king bastard!

MAAHI:

Veeru is furious.

It was different in the morning; we were lucky: Ms Kerkar in the Junta House was quite helpful. A lot of credit should also go to Veeru for making Ms Kerkar believe our made-up story by telling it with amazing conviction. Frankly, I would have believed him too; anyone would have believed him. And so he had managed – despite not giving a name – to persuade Ms Kerkar to take him through the list of accidents on 21st July that had involved a girl close to me in age.

And then from luck we slid into lucklessness; none of those girls could have been the living version of me. It also seemed God had developed a twisted sense of humour that day; the three major religions of India were represented equally in the accidents.

To hope that we would discover who I was at the first place we went to was I guess too much to hope for. I wasn't that lucky obviously; otherwise I wouldn't be…

I sighed. It was so difficult not to pity one's self and not to wish for a greater amount of luck.

And it seemed whatever bit of luck we had in the morning had definitely run out by the afternoon. After being made to wait for almost three hours at the Quepem office, we met a grumpy man who was least interested in listening to Veeru's story or in helping him find his missing cousin. Curtly he told Veeru that he had no more information than what we got at Junta House, and made it clear that he would like Veeru to leave immediately. One got the impression that if the man had his way, missing cousins and people searching for them would be outlawed.

And now after the meeting is over, it's plain from Veeru's face that he is boiling with anger.

I try to calm him down.

"The guy said he had important work that we were interrupting," I said defending the man. "Maybe that was true. And he knew he could give us no more information than what we already had, so there was no point talking further."

"It's not about the information, Maahi!" Veeru fumes to me through his mobile as people walk by him. "It's about the way he treated the whole thing. As if he didn't give a shit whether someone lived or died!"

I shake my head.

"What if it's not exactly that?" I argue. "He deals with such requests every day. Missing sons, missing daughters, fathers, mothers, brothers, sisters… A cousin would be a level down for him, if anything. Maybe the only way he can cope with all that is by not caring."

Veeru smiles feebly. Says maybe I am right, but he is not feeling very forgiving right now. Almost the whole day is gone and we are nowhere.

"It's ok," I reply to console him. "We have made definite progress. We now definitely know where I am *not*. I am not there in the records of the transport department. That takes care of ninety percent of road accidents."

He is surprised. "How can you be so calm, Maahi? When we have just seven days more?"

I sigh. How do I tell him I am not calm? That I am very scared.

But I can't show it now. I hate to see him upset. And I can't upset him more by getting upset myself. Right now, I have to hold the ground, and hold it firmly.

"Let's go to the Margao hospital," I tell him.

VEERU:

Till now, I had not really thought about the scenario in which I failed to help Maahi find her unknown lover and she got trapped here with all her pain. Thinking about failure was not easy. I had heard from ma'am and Maahi words like *pain, escape, trapped, eternity, oblivion, nothingness* and so on; but never before having encountered a ghost trapped on earth, I had only a very hazy idea what the words meant. The whole thing was a like a dark, forbidding hall to me, a place in which you didn't know what you would find, and so I had not been very willing to enter it; I had let the unknown remain unknown.

To know more, to know what was the *actual cost of failure*, would have been a painful burden. I was much more comfortable believing I would surely succeed in my mission than understand in entirety the task I had taken upon my shoulders.

But no more. Day one was almost over, our search had turned up nothing, and it was time to enter the dark hall, however threatening it seemed.

"Suppose if we don't find Hrithik, what happens after seven days?" I asked Maahi as we rode to the Hospicio Margao, one of the three big hospitals in Goa where almost all the emergency cases were brought. The other two hospitals were GMCH and Asilo Mapusa, and they were next on the list of the places where we planned to go and search.

Maahi kept silent.

"Maahi?" I asked again.

I still didn't get any answer, so I stopped the bike on the side of the road. I wasn't going till I got my answer. I looked around. There was no one close to us; the pretence of talking on the cellphone wasn't necessary.

"I want to know, Maahi," I said persisting. "What really happens?"

… … …

"MAAHI!"

"I don't really… know," she replied softly at last.

"Shall we get down and talk?"

"Okay."

We got down, I put the bike on the side-stand, and we walked under the shade of a mango tree.

I stood a little away from the tree facing it. Maahi, I assumed, was standing between me and the tree. "You said if that happens, you would get trapped here forever," I said. "Didn't you?"

She sighed. "Maybe… yes. I don't know."

"But—"

"Really, I don't know. Just that Asmi ma'am told me that… *could* happen."

"But you aren't sure?"

"No. Ma'am was… I mean, I felt even ma'am wasn't sure. I think she had seen a case like mine for the first time. She was somewhat guessing."

I nodded. "Anyway what does 'forever' mean? Till the end of time?"

"End of time?"

"I mean for how much time will you be trapped? When do you find freedom… according to ma'am?"

"Why do you want to know?"

"I just want to!"

"Please Veeru. Let it—"

"Maahi, why can't you tell me? It's simple—"

"It's not simple," she cut me short quietly.

I ignored her.

"Till *when*? That's all I am asking. Is it till the time you would have ordinarily lived? Till human beings cease to exist? Till the earth gets destroyed? Till the universe folds back into a point? What is—"

"Stop it, Veeru!"

Suddenly, she was shrieking at me. "Don't you understand? I don't know and I don't want to know!"

Startled, I fell back almost a meter. She repeated less harshly: "I don't *want* to know!"

I could hear her breathing hard. Was she angry? Yes, I felt she *was*… very angry. I would never have admitted it, but I was quite scared myself now. I didn't know how ghosts behaved when they were angry.

We stood there, without words, for a few moments.

"You are scared." She was the first one to break the silence with a matter of fact statement.

I had forgotten. Not only could she see my face, but also read my mind sometimes.

"No… I—"

"I am really sorry, I forgot I was a ghost," she interrupted me in a small voice, sounding unhappy. "I shouldn't have yelled at you. I am sorry."

Oh shit! Quickly, I tried to make up for my stupidity. "It's ok," I said coming closer with haste.

"It was me who was at fault. I pushed you too far. And I am not scared."

"Don't be afraid please," she went on pleading despite my apology. "I am sorry. I don't know what came over me, but I would never hurt you. Believe me."

My ears burned with embarrassment. How, even for a moment, could I…

"I know, Maahi," I said moving closer till I could hear her breathe just inches ahead of me. "I know. I am not scared. See… see how close we are. If I move a step closer, I will knock my nose into yours," I whispered to her grinning. "I am not at all scared."

I actually wanted to do that. I had an intense desire to knock my nose against hers.

She was silent for a few moments. Then she said: "Would you, Veeru?"

"What?"

"You said you will knock your nose against mine. Can you?"

I couldn't understand what she meant. "I guess…" I said tentatively. "I mean I—"

"No, you cannot." She cut me. "You cannot, even if you want to. You will simply go through me. You know that. I am formless, invisible. I am thin air. You can't see me, you can't touch me, you can't knock your nose against mine. That's why you are scared of me, because I am thin air. Because I am nothing. Scared of me even if I can't hurt you, and will never hurt you even if I could. But you will still be scared of me because you can't help it. Because the living can't help being scared of invisible ghosts however close to them they are. We are the others. And that's the truth!"

"Maahi—"

"I just knocked my nose against yours. Did you feel it? No, you didn't feel it. And you would *never* feel it. And that's also the truth."

"What happened, Maahi?"

"Nothing."

Suddenly I heard what seemed like a sob. Was she crying? My heart rose in my mouth. Had I made her cry?

"Maahi?"

Silence. Just another sob.

"Maahi… please, what happened, Maahi?"

"Nothing," she repeated. And then a third sob.

"Are you crying? Why are you crying?"

"Don't talk to me in that voice," she said, her voice cracking. "Please don't." And suddenly she broke into a series of distressing sobs.

What voice? What did I say now?

I gazed at the thin air where she stood as she went on crying. I didn't know what to do to stop those sobs. I wanted to see her, badly. Why was she crying? I wanted to hold her, comfort her. Pull her to me and tell her I am sorry with more than just words. But there was nothing I could do except listen to the sobs helplessly.

How do you stop thin air from crying?

MAAHI:

It's his voice. I couldn't bear the note in it – the note of solicitude, the note of care. And I broke down. Why does he have to use that… that note? Especially after making me feel I was going to kill him or something. He looked that scared. I felt so bad. What did I do to get that emotion? Nothing! I just yelled at him. Yelled like any other girl would because he just wouldn't understand that I don't want to even think about seven days later. I was myself scared and then he gets even more scared when I yell at him. What is my fault, except that I am a ghost and he can't see me? Does that mean I would hurt him or kill him because I am a little angry?

I don't want to talk about what would happen seven days later. Why can't he understand that? I don't clearly know the answer myself and I am afraid. I am trying to be brave and strong but it's so difficult. I had almost succeeded and then he had to pig-headedly bring the topic up. I want to break his pig-head! How much time? Why does he want to know? What good would it do? I don't know myself. If we failed, it could be a really long time, ma'am had said. When I asked what was really long, ma'am herself didn't know. Could be tens, hundreds, even thousands of years. If ghosts didn't find oblivion in the first fourteen days, then they wandered till one sudden day, a scene or words or melody struck some powerful chord in our memory and aroused strong enough emotions to liberate us. But it was a chance event and could take any number of years. Yes, theoretically it could even be till the universe folded back into itself.

I don't want to think about it. It's frightening to think of being trapped for that long, with the pain. And I don't want him to look at me with so much tenderness. I know he is sorry to make me cry and wants to hold me and comfort me. He tells me he wants to knock my nose with his. Makes me want to cry even more, makes me want to live. Makes me want to stop being invisible, want to stop being thin air. I want to be touched, I want to be felt. I want my nose knocked. I want to be human.

I want to be alive. No, I can't wish for those things. They won't happen. And I can't stop myself from crying.

"Don't look at me like that," I tell him and turn around to look the other way. I don't want to look at his face. It makes me cry. I know I have to stop crying. And I have to stop wishing for impossible things. We have to leave. We don't have time.

I control myself with some effort, turn my head and look at him sideways. He is still looking at me like that. Why? *Stop making me cry you idiot*, I want to yell at him. I want to punch him. In that big nose of his. If I break his nose, then he won't be able to knock it anywhere. Stupid!

Annoyed, I turn back to tell him that. That's when, before I can open my mouth, suddenly, he cries out my name.

VEERU:

I could swear I had seen her hair swirl by my face. I could swear it. It was for a thousandth of a second, just a glimpse. Not even a glimpse but the tiniest of flickers I should say. Like being wet by a solitary, tiny drop from the sky on a sunny day. You could swear it was a raindrop. No one may believe you, but you could swear it had happened. I could swear I had seen Maahi.

I thought so. And so I cried out her name, "Maahi!"

She was startled. "What?"

"I saw you."

"What?"

"I said I *saw* you."

"Saw me?"

Her voice was disbelieving but normal. She wasn't crying anymore. I was relieved.

"Yes! Saw you. Your hair at least."

"What are you talking about?"

Yes, I know it sounded crazy. But so what? It was the truth.

"I know it sounds crazy, but…" Then I had an idea. If I was right, her hair had just swirled past me. She must be then…

"Okay, tell me right now were you like turning towards me… or away from me? Were you?"

She was silent.

My heart jumped. "Were you?" I repeated.

"Yes… I was," she said slowly.

"See! I saw it."

"But how can you see me?"

She was still not convinced. "You must have imagined..." She paused. "Don't tell me you are saying all this to just stop my crying? I'll kill you!"

"No, I am not!"

"Then why—"

"Ok… you think I imagined this? Fine. But then how did I imagine that you were turning towards me? How did I know exactly that's what happened?"

She didn't reply.

"I didn't imagine it Maahi. Trust me, I *saw* you. Just for the tiniest moment, but I saw you."

"But I am a ghost!"

"So what… I can still hear you. If I can hear you, why can't I even see you?"

"That's different. Ma'am said you could hear me if you believed in me, believed I existed. But she never said anything about you being able to see me."

"Maybe ma'am doesn't know."

"She would. If this could happen, she would have told us," Maahi was obstinate.

"But…"

Then I remembered something. "Hold on. I think ma'am knows. She did once talk about me seeing you."

"No, if… she did? When?"

"Remember… she said while introducing you that you would be the loveliest ghost I would see if I ever saw you. She did talk about me seeing you."

"Don't make things up!"

"I am not making anything up. I clearly remember. You want to ask ma'am?"

"No," she said in a small voice. "I don't. And I am not doubting you. It's just that—"

"Maahi," I cut her gently. "It's not about doubt. If it's true… I am just so excited. I can see you! Even if it's just a flicker, I can see you. Imagine!" I paused. "And I want to see you. I *so* want to see you." I paused again. "Don't you want me to see you?"

She said slowly. "Yes…"

MAAHI:

He says he saw me. Though it was just a flicker as my hair swirled by his face. He looks so excited and happy. I don't know. I am a ghost, how can he see me? Ma'am never said anything like this could happen.

Yet he *does* know that I was turning back towards him when he thought he saw me. And he did cry out my name. And I wasn't even talking then. How could he know that unless…

I don't like this. I am a ghost, he is living. He shouldn't be able to see me. Am I becoming like him? Or is he becoming like me? I don't like this.

"Maahi?"

"Yes."

"What are you thinking?"

"Nothing."

"I know you are thinking something. I can feel it."

"No… nothing."

"Shall I call ma'am and ask her about this? If I can see you?"

What can I say? I don't want him to but…

"Yes."

So he calls up ma'am and tells her he thinks he saw a glimpse of me a little while ago and asks her if that is possible. The speaker phone is on. We have silence for a few moments. Then Ma'am asks him:

"Are you sure?"

"Yes, I think so. Maahi was turning towards me, so her hair swirled by my face and that's what I saw. I couldn't have known Maahi was turning unless I really saw what I saw."

"Is Maahi there?"

"Yes, she is with me and listening to you. We are on the speaker phone."

"Maahi," ma'am asks me. "What do you think? Did Veeru really see you?"

"I… I think so," I say with hesitation. For some reason, I just don't like this discussion. I don't know why, but I just don't.

"So… can this happen?" Veeru asks Ma'am, his eyes shining.

"It's possible," Ma'am says slowly. "It has happened, but very rarely."

"See!" Veeru jerks his head from the phone towards me. "I told you! When I—"

"What did you exactly see?" Ma'am cuts him.

"Just a tiny glimpse of her hair. Like it was a flicker on the television."

"Nothing more?"

"No… that's all." He pauses. "Will I see more?"

Before ma'am can speak, I interrupt her, "Veeru, we are getting late. It's four-thirty already!"

More than the time, I am worried about bringing the discussion to an end. I *don't* want to know how he can see me.

"Hold on," Veeru is unmoved. "Will I see more?" he asks ma'am again.

"I don't know," ma'am says. "I don't know what makes seeing a ghost possible, so I can't tell. It may not be good also," ma'am concludes in a worried voice.

I knew it! I knew something was not good about this whole thing!

"Why is it not good?" Veeru asks.

"I don't know," ma'am says. "Just a hunch."

But Veeru is adamant after our call is over. There can be nothing bad about this, he declares. How can there be anything bad in being able to see a friend?

"Something is telling me I'll see more of you very soon," he tells me as we get on the bike to continue on our way to the hospital.

"Maybe your nose."

Something is telling me the same too. But after my bad feeling and ma'am's worried voice, I dearly hope Veeru is wrong.

VEERU:

I couldn't understand it. I thought Maahi would be very happy that I could see her, but it seemed she was not. She sounded worried, unwilling to believe what had happened. Even ma'am wasn't happy when we called her up. It was a rare event she said, and perhaps not a good thing.

Not a good thing? Why shouldn't it be good? What was bothering them? Was there something they weren't telling me?

Anyway, I was the only one among the three very happy to see the glimpse of a ghost's hair. And if ma'am was to be believed, the glimpse of a very lovely ghost's lovely hair (quite quite unlike the terrifying hair of the ghost from *The Ring*).

I know it's a little stupid to be over the moon just because for the tiniest of moments, I saw some hair. Maybe very stupid. But hair would do for now; I was sure that in sometime I would see more. For example, it was quite probable that I would soon see the nose that I wanted to knock my own nose upon and which action Maahi had challenged me I couldn't.

Well, she may be right about the knocking part. But I still would get to see that nose; and whatever ma'am or Maahi may feel about me seeing a ghostly nose, they won't be able to stop me.

Now and then, I had wondered what Maahi had looked like. I had tried to picture the face behind that lovely voice, a voice that in the plane had sounded as if someone was singing songs from far away calling to you to come to them. And asking you not to leave.

Aaj jaane ki zidd na karo.

But no matter how much I tried, I was never able to imagine her. She had just remained that voice, a voice that I wanted to fall in love with. Or had I already fallen in love with?

I didn't know. But I surely did know that I badly wanted to see my Miss Dark Chocolaty. Her nose too.

MAAHI:

It's about four-fifty when we reach Hospicio Margao. We are late by a few minutes we are told. The clerk who has the records we want has left and we are asked to come tomorrow.

Veeru is unhappy to hear this and begins apologizing to me for making us late. I stop him; I have a feeling our coming here earlier wouldn't have made a difference. Something tells me whatever happened with me didn't happen in Goa.

Seven days are gone, seven days left. And I am desperate to leave and to find my way to nothingness. I am a ghost. I shouldn't be here. I don't belong here, this is not my place.

Inexplicably, the pain inside me has gone down. I don't know why, but it's slowly lessening. It's almost bearable now. I mean the times Veeru made me worried or mad, I wasn't even aware it was there. I have to ask ma'am the reason. Sometime I will.

The pain has lessened and I should be happy, but I am not. The intense pain had given me purpose, a reason to get out. I had more than a reason; I was almost desperate to find oblivion. To just get out.

Now, I almost don't mind staying longer if not for… Yes, I am still desperate to go, but the 'why' has changed. It's not the pain anymore that pushes me towards nothingness. It's Veeru. I am afraid for him. Why is he beginning to see me suddenly?

Why does he talk to me so affectionately? Why does he look at me like that?

It's my fault. I shouldn't have cried in front of him, I shouldn't have been weak. I shouldn't have touched the tenderness in him. I shouldn't have asked for his help.

But I can't help it. I can't help wishing for… I may not be living, but I still have those emotions. I wish to be cared for, to be protected, to be held, to be touched. To have my nose knocked.

I don't know how my life went by, but should even death be so difficult?

VEERU:

After we came back from Hospicio Margao, that we had reached too late, all thanks to me, I took a nap while Maahi said she would roam in the area close to the hotel. When I got up, it was almost eight. Thinking Maahi was not in the room I decided to take a shower and took off my t-shirt. I had just opened the button of my jeans as well when I heard a giggle.

Maahi was in the room!

"F**k!" I said on autopilot, buttoned my jeans back and hastened to put on my t-shirt.

Maahi was still giggling when I asked her, "When did you come?"

"You have a nice body," was her non-sequitur.

I was expecting something like that. "Don't lie," I told her. "I don't. Anyway, when did you come?"

"I am not lying. *I* like it." She paused. "I came a while back. You had already slept."

"But how did you come in? The door was locked. You walk through walls?"

"I teleported."

"That's cool!"

I *knew* it. So this was the second ghost-like power that Maahi exhibited. After mindreading. (But was mindreading among ghostly powers? I wasn't sure).

"And I am sorry I didn't knock," she went on. "I can't."

"I know. It's okay."

"You were taking your clothes off," she giggled. "Why did you stop?"

"Ya! That reminds me…" It had suddenly occurred to me she couldn't be let off so easily. "Why didn't you warn me you were here when I started taking them off?" I asked.

"Why should I? Who minds free striptease on a Friday evening?"

"Today's Thursday," I reminded her sweetly. "And if this continues, I will have to get you your own room, Miss."

"How will that help? I can teleport here anytime."

Now that was solid logic. I had nothing to say to that.

"And I can teleport anytime into the bathroom too," she finished, destroying my threat with a chuckle.

"Please don't," I pleaded, suddenly feeling defenceless. I hoped ghosts didn't have superman-like powers too, to see through clothes and all. I didn't want to be Lois Lane to Maahi's Superman!

"What do I get?"

Huh? I frowned. What was this? Why should I give her anything?

"Why should you get anything?"

"Because… you know… teleporting into the bathroom is still an option."

I capitulated; the threat was formidable.

"What do you want?"

"Go topless to the shower."

"Whaaaaat!"

"You heard me. Remember the alternative? It's worse."

She was right. The alternative was much much worse. After dallying for a couple of minutes which was of no help, I took off my t-shirt with a grumble. "This is like… blackmail."

"You bet it is," she shot back with a giggle as I walked with crossed arms to the shower.

"Flagrant misuse of my ghostly powers it is.

"And I like it," she ended with some more giggles.

While showering, I called out her name deliberately to check where she was. She got what I was doing. "Don't worry Mr, Shy," she yelled back from the room. "I am not peeping in. I am right here."

After I finished, we went downstairs to the hotel restaurant to get me some coffee since I wasn't feeling hungry. I could have asked for room service, and Maahi did suggest that, but I chose to go down because I also had a hidden agenda; I wanted to try out an experiment without Maahi knowing it.

In that cause, I made her sit on a strategically chosen chair in the main restaurant while I went to the adjoining café to get my coffee. The chair on which Maahi sat was placed such that you could watch from the café a person sitting on it without getting seen yourself; the connecting door hid you nicely if you stood at a certain spot close to the door.

After I had got my coffee, I stood at the spot looking at the chair where I had left Maahi sitting. Since no one could see Maahi and the restaurant was mostly empty, I knew I wouldn't face any problem gazing at the chair. It would just appear to people as if I was thinking something while sipping coffee.

Actually, I wasn't just looking at the chair; I was staring at it with all the concentration I could muster. And at the same time, I was praying hard. Praying hard to God to help me see Maahi.

But nothing happened despite all my staring and praying. I didn't even see the flicker of her hair that I had seen last time. I almost gave up on the experiment, even worrying whether Maahi had left the chair (she could well be standing right next to me laughing at my antics).

Then I changed my mind and decided to give the experiment a second shot – the last one for the time-being. I recalled the emotion I had felt when I saw Maahi's hair a few hours ago – I remembered the extreme anxiety and remorse at making her cry, and the deep desire to stop the sobs somehow and make up for them. And I also remembered I had wanted to touch her. I had wanted that intensely; wanted to take her in my arms and comfort her till she stopped crying.

I closed my eyes.

Maahi and I.

We stood next to the mango tree. We started arguing. She got angry and yelled at me. I got scared and drew back. She got hurt. I hastily came closer and told her I had come so close I could knock my nose against hers. She challenged me saying I couldn't because she was a ghost, and ghosts and people, however close they were, couldn't knock noses.

There was silence.

And then I heard Maahi again. I heard her crying next to the mango tree. She was turned away from me. I could see the back of her head, her long, cascading hair, I could hear the sobs.

Once again I had the intense desire to pull her into my arms. To comfort her, stop her from crying. Say I am sorry with my arms.

I did that this time. I put my arms out to fold her into them.

Then I opened my eyes.

MAAHI:

While Veeru is taking his nap, I decide to visit Asmi ma'am to ask her the questions I have. Why is my pain slowly lessening? How did Veeru see my hair even if it was just a glimpse?

I am sure ma'am didn't tell us all when we had called her. Whatever the reason, it was clear she was not happy to know that Veeru could see me.

But Asmi ma'am is not there when I teleport myself to her garden. The house is empty. I wait for her for about twenty minutes before I return deciding to revisit her later.

Veeru has dropped into a deep sleep when I come back. He must be very tired. He had got up quite early in the morning to catch the flight, and after that he was taking me all over Goa the whole day. We would have easily ridden more than a hundred kilometres since morning.

I sit by his pillow. He is sleeping on his side, his right arm flung away, his left curled up on another pillow. I watch him sleep. He looks so calm, peaceful sleeping. I have the desire to put my hand in his hair and ruffle it. I watch him for a long time, my hand moving through his hair unable to ruffle a strand. Even his hair is calm. Does it mind a ghost's attempt to disturb it?

I think about myself. What was I like when I was alive? Was I calm like Veeru's hair? Was I stormy? I wish I was a calm person when I was alive. I haven't had a moment of peace since I died. Ma'am told me not to worry though. If everything went well, peace will come to me soon. A peace to last forever.

And yet… once again I have the disquieting feeling. Do I want that peace anymore?

I look at Veeru. I think tracing my finger on his cheek that I want Veeru's kind of peace. Which lasts for a while, not forever. But then I am not someone who has a choice.

Suddenly, I feel tired. The tiredness of being without choice. I lie down and curl by Veeru's side on the edge of the bed. I snuggle close to him feeling secure. Even if I can't touch him, his nearness is enough. I close my eyes… and slowly drift off.

I hear waves. A man calling me from far away. It's in a language I don't know though the voice sounds familiar. I see golden hair. I hear the roar of a truck. An elephant's leg decorated in intricate patterns with white. A garland of flowers. Bells ringing. Children laughing. Glimpse of a street. Cacophony of traffic. Darkness. Tables and chairs. The smell of food. A bottle of wine. Glass broken on the floor. Wine everywhere. Blood everywhere. Darkness. Moon in the sky. Sun in the sky. A huge golden ball in the sky. Smell of incense. Light streaming through the trees. Top of a tree. The same voice laughing. "Don't be afraid, I am here." And then I am falling. Falling and falling. I scream.

I wake up with a start and look around. I am still lying next to Veeru. He is still sleeping.

And then the realization hits me. Was that sleep? Did I just sleep for the first time in seven days?

VEERU:

She shimmered and flickered as if she was made of a constellation of a thousand stars. Gazing straight, with eyes that were lost to the world. I stopped breathing. She was lovely, so lovely and her nose that I wanted to knock, curved a little.

Suddenly, she turned to look my way, and I started feeling as if she had caught me stealing. Our eyes met. We gazed at each other for a moment. Hers had confusion in them. Mine had…

I realised I had fallen in love with a ghost.

MAAHI:

I am sitting in the hotel restaurant while Veeru is gone to the adjoining café to get coffee for himself. Left to myself, I think about the dream I just had in the room (Was it a dream? It must be right?) till it seems to me that Veeru is gone a really long time. I turn my head to look at the connecting doors and I am surprised to see him standing close to the doors. Why is he standing there? How long has he been standing there?

Then I am even more surprised. Why is he looking at me with wide eyes? As if he had seen a ghost?

I know I am a ghost. But how…

Our eyes meet. I realise he is looking at me with a strange… intensity? Why?

And then I understand quickly; sharp claws of fear grip my heart.

Is he seeing me? Is he really seeing me?

VEERU:

I knew that Maahi wouldn't be happy if she came to know that I could see her. So I pretended I still couldn't see her; and when I talked to her, I focused everywhere except on her eyes. Sometimes it was on her ears. Sometimes it was on her neck. Sometimes on her cheeks. Sometimes on her mouth. Sometimes on her hair. And often on the tip of her nose.

The tip of her nose was my favourite place. Of course, thinking about various ways in which I could knock on it added spice when I focused on it.

After I finished my coffee, we decided to go for a walk on the beach. We walked to the south away from the crowd (which was a small one, July being off season) so that I could talk to Maahi without either pretending to talk into my mobile or looking nutty.

For quite some time, we walked silently. I didn't want to say anything; I was just content to glance at her from time to time, elated to confirm each time that I could really see her. Though she still shimmered, with each glance she grew more and more substantial. As if each glance was pulling her, the unearthly girl, down to earth and close to me. She also kept silent, and I wondered what she was thinking.

I got to know soon. When we were fairly alone and the periodic noise of breaking of waves was almost the only sound we could hear, she asked me suddenly: "Why were you staring at me like that in the restaurant?"

I was jolted. Had she caught me looking at her? Had she read my mind again? Did she know?

Maybe she had read my mind. That was most likely, but I wasn't going to give up easily. Anyway, she couldn't be sure if she had read me right. I pretended to not understand her. "Staring at you? When?"

"In the restaurant. While you were standing near the connecting doors. I saw you staring at me."

"Oh that!" I had to tell a lie now. I couldn't help it.

"I was not staring at *you*," I told her. "I guess I was just… staring."

"Just… staring? Meaning?"

"I mean I didn't *know* at that time I was staring… at you or anything. I was just remembering something. Did you feel that I was staring at you?"

"Yes."

"Oh… sorry!" I paused, and then gave a short laugh. "But how can I stare at you when I can't even see you… yet." I paused again. "I wish I could though."

"I don't know. I just thought you were staring. What were you remembering so deeply?"

I knew this was going to come. I sighed. Time for some more lies. But I didn't want to go ahead without a last try at digging my heels. "Do I *have* to tell that?"

Maahi was adamant. "You don't have to. But I would like to know."

So I told her: "I was remembering the last time I was here. Next to those doors, I had a fight with someone."

My lie was not an absolute lie. The incident had indeed happened even if I hadn't remembered it.

Maahi was silent for a few moments. Then she asked: "Was the fight with the girl you told ma'am about in the morning?"

"Yes."

So Maahi remembered my face-off with ma'am. And I couldn't help laughing remembering the way Ma'am had steamrolled me in that face-off.

"Why are you laughing?"

"I remembered the way ma'am royally kicked my ass in the morning. I would have loved to put Gautami in front of her. It would have been epic."

Maahi chuckled. "Ma'am is a character, isn't she?"

"Yup... totally. A woman of original mind. I still have no clue how she played with our website the way she did! Whatever technology she used, we never knew anything as kick-ass as that existed!"

"Hmm... Her name was Gautami?"

Gautami? S**t! I had said the name without thinking. And Maahi had caught it. This was definitely not the direction I wanted our conversation to go. "Yes..." I said with reluctance.

"Nice name."

"Maybe."

"I know Veerupakshya means God Shiva." Maahi didn't seem to be either getting or paying attention to my tone. "What does Gautami mean?"

"No idea!"

"Come on!"

I sighed. "Gautam I know means the enlightened one. It was the name of Buddha too. Gautami... I really don't know."

"And you never found out? Don't lie!"

Why had she got to push it? I definitely didn't want to remember Gautami now. Especially with her.

"I am waiting."

She wasn't letting it go. "Fine... It's a variation on Godavari."

"The river?"

"Yes. And it also means someone who removes darkness. And it also means the wife of sage Gautam." Let her take all of that and be happy. "And it also—"

Maahi spoke in between, "*And* someone was claiming he didn't know the meaning of Gautami." She chuckled. "What a shameless liar you are, Veeru!"

"I know that," I told her. "And even *you* know that. Remember you already complemented me on my lying?"

"Huh… When did I do that?"

"At the Junta office in the morning?"

She frowned trying to remember.

"When I told Mr Kerkar our cooked-up story?" I went on.

Now her brows cleared. "Oh… yes! I remember now. I am sorry." She looked sheepish. "You didn't mind that, did you?"

"It's ok. I know I am a good liar." I paused. "Gautami thought so too. Sometimes it helps, so I don't mind being one."

And thank god Maahi had no idea how true that statement was! My lying skills were *so* helping me right now.

"Yes… it definitely helps," she said echoing me. "I am so sorry I said that in the morning."

"I *said* it's ok."

She smiled. "Better let me change the topic. How did Gautami break your heart?"

Great change of topic! Aaarghhh…

"She didn't. Or at least she thought she didn't. Actually, it wasn't quite clear who broke whose heart. There was major confusion and difference of opinion between us on that topic."

Maahi turned her head towards me. I kept looking straight, but I could see her eyes were shining. "Sounds like an interesting story."

"Sure. But which I have no intention of telling."

"Why?"

Hello! Did I even need to explain? "Remember? It was you who stopped Ma'am from questioning me in the morning?" I said admonishing Maahi. "Now you're going on and on yourself!"

"Ok…" She sighed upturning her lips. "No Gautami-Veeru love-hate story for an interested ghost."

She paused. "Shall we talk about Ghazal?"

Was she doing this on purpose? She must be doing this on purpose. "Shall I wring your neck?"

"You can't see me," she replied at once. "Can you? Then how will you wring my neck?"

If Maahi thought I could fall for such an easy bait, I was going to disappoint her. "I can't see you. But I can definitely hear you," I told her. "Hear you very well. And necks lie close to mouths. The distance I am sure can be estimated with fair accuracy."

"Yes. But only in people. I am a ghost. How do you know what's the right distance for ghosts?"

"How does that matter?" I shot back. "Unless becoming a ghost increases the length of your neck and you become like a… giraffe?"

"No, ghosts have necks like…" She stopped abruptly. "Wait! Ghosts… giraffes… the words remind me of someone," she said, pretending to think deeply.

"Remind? Who?"

"Ghazal."

"Maahi!"

She went on with a straight and serious face:

"What can I do? It's the sound of 'g', I am telling you! Giraffes… ghosts… Ghazal. They all sound so alike!"

"Yes!" I said nodding. "They sound very alike. And Ghazal I am sure is the ghost of a giraffe having a very long neck which will be nice to wring! Happy?"

"Why don't you like Ghazal? She was such a sweet, pretty girl."

To hell with Ghazal! You are far sweeter and prettier! I wanted to tell her.

But that's not what I said.

"I am not particularly against Ghazal. I am against all girls whose names start with 'g'. Ghazal… Ganga… Gautami… all of them. The whole lot!"

"Ghazal has nothing whatsoever to do with Gautami!" Maahi exclaimed.

"I know. And I will have nothing whatsoever to do with girls whose names start with 'g'." I paused.

"And now shall we turn back?" I said indicating a small creek which lay on our path about thirty metres ahead. "I don't think we can cross that."

But Maahi wasn't letting go. "Don't change the topic, Veeru! Take me… I am a *girl* ghost. That's a double 'g' for you! So?"

"So?"

"So will you have nothing whatsoever to do with me?"

"Don't be ridiculous, Maahi!" I was beginning to feel angry.

"Am *I* the one being ridiculous?"

"Yes, you are the one!" Perhaps knowing she was right was making me angrier.

"Why don't you just answer my question?" Her quiet voice had a faint mocking edge to it.

My temper flared at her tone. "What question will I answer?" I half shouted.

"Will you have nothing whatsoever to do with me?"

"Does your name begin with 'g'?" I yelled at her this time.

"How do you know?"

"What?" I yelled again despite getting her meaning perfectly.

"How do you know it doesn't, Veeru? What if we discover it does?"

I had no answer to that. And I couldn't keep on saying 'what'.

"What if it does, Veeru?" she asked softly again. "Will you stop helping me?"

"No."

"Whatever my name is?"

"It wouldn't matter," I said, quietly this time.

"Yes…" she nodded. "It wouldn't matter. Would it?"

We had almost reached the creek. I desperately wanted to talk about something else.

"The creek has come," I said. "Let's turn back."

Maahi nodded and we turned back. We walked in silence for some time. Then Maahi turned her head towards me.

"I don't know if I have the right to say this…" She paused. "But I may not be with you for more than seven days. And you and ma'am are perhaps the only two friends I will have in this strange, short life of a ghost, and I know I couldn't hope for better ones. So I will say it anyway. I hope you will forgive me if what I say is hurting…"

She paused and waited. I didn't say anything.

"Will you?

I nodded. "Anything."

She stopped and turned towards me fully. I stopped too and turned. I stared at her lips, afraid to look into her eyes.

The lips moved. "Gautami's gone, Veeru. And she may never come back."

She had beautiful lips. Everything about her was beautiful. And she was going away. I swallowed. "I know."

"You have to move on."

I kept silent.

"Will you? You are not my boyfriend but you are my only friend who is a boy. I want you to be happy when I am gone."

A simple statement. I nodded, and turned my head away from her. I guess she wanted to make me laugh but my eyes were beginning to water and I didn't want her to see that. I started walking. I kept walking. The waves kept crashing against the sand. Maahi kept shimmering beside me, reminding me of her words.

I want you to be happy when I am gone.

Gone? Happy? How could I tell her that I had already moved on? How could I tell her the wonderful irony was the girl I had moved on to was not going to be with me for more than seven days and I could do nothing about it except carry on fulfilling my promise of doing my best to help her go away? How could I be happy when she was gone?

Suddenly, Maahi stopped. "I have stopped, Veeru," she told me. "You go ahead. I want to be alone for some time. I will join you in the room."

"What happened?"

"Nothing. I just want to surf on the waves for a while. And you can't join me. Better go on."

I nodded and kept walking. I understood. She wanted to be alone.

She turned and walked on to the sea. Walked on and on over the water. The shimmering light moved away from me amidst the crashing of the waves, growing fainter and fainter till it was lost into the heart of an infinite darkness.

MAAHI:

He can see me. I am sure of that now. When I stopped the first time and turned towards him, he stopped too and turned towards me. Since I hadn't said anything, how could he know I had stopped?

He is lying to me. Why? I think I know, but I don't want to know. And I am afraid. I don't want to hurt him.

I have to talk to ma'am alone. I have to find out what all of this means. I have to find a way to not hurt him.

We start walking and then I stop and tell him I want to be alone for some time. He asks why and I lie that it's because I want to surf the waves and he can't join me. He nods and walks on. I think he knows that I am lying and I feel bad but I can't help it.

I walk to the sea and keep going over the water. I walk backwards watching Veeru amble till he disappears into the crowd of people far away. Then I turn around and keep going, faster and faster till the shoreline is just a collection of hazy blips. And then not even that.

I am in the middle of the sea. I stay there for some time with my eyes closed. I soak in the feelings that I have – of the vastness of the sea, of the vaster earth, of being here. Of being alive in a peculiar way.

I am here and now, even if for a little while.

And far away someone who is helping me be alive, this alive, loves me… My heart constricts. Why does it have to be like this? It's not… fair.

I clench my fists, focus my mind and teleport to ma'am's house.

VEERU:

When I came back to the hotel, it was about ten-fifteen. I was in no mood to eat anything, so I went straight up to the room and lay down on the bed, waiting for Maahi. Now and then I would call out her name to check if she had returned, but I was greeted by silence.

After some time, it became impossible to lie still. I got up and checked the time. It was almost eleven. Where was she? How long did it take to surf the waves if she was surfing at all? I knew there was no question of her drowning or anything, yet I couldn't help feeling afraid.

I mean why did she want to be alone? Did she just leave without telling me? My heart said that wasn't possible, but I didn't know anything about ghosts. Maybe they were volatile. Maybe even if she didn't show it, she had got angry because I shouted at her. Maybe she… did she *know*?

If she had left, she would have gone to ma'am's house. There was no other place. I decided to call up Ma'am.

Just before tapping the number, I stopped. It would look so stupid. Maahi had clearly told me she was staying behind to surf. (How did ghosts surf anyway?)

Anyway, wouldn't ma'am ask why couldn't Maahi surf for an hour or two without me getting hyper? These were the last of her days on earth and maybe it was the last time she was surfing. Why couldn't she surf for as long as she wanted? Who was I to get so worried? She could take perfect care of herself. Why was I getting so anxious?

"Maahi!" I called again. And again I heard nothing but silence. Her absence was excruciating.

I went out into the corridor and started walking. It was better than lying down. I walked and walked till I got very tired and couldn't walk anymore. I came back into the room and looked at my watch. Twelve-fifteen. Where was Maahi? It was almost two and a half hours since I had left her on the beach. Now I was beginning to get scared. This was too long a time.

I debated if I should I call ma'am. But what if Maahi was really surfing and had taken a liking to it? What would I tell Maahi when she returned? What if she got angry?

There was nothing else to be done. I had to go back to the beach.

MAAHI:

When I come back to the room, Veeru is not there. I am surprised. Where could he have gone? It's almost two-thirty! I look in the restaurant, but it is closed. I am wondering what to do when it strikes me that, of course, he has gone back to the beach to look for me.

I teleport myself to the beach, and sure enough, he is sitting close to the creek looking at the sea. He is scanning the horizon, searching for me.

I look around. It's dark and totally quiet. There is no one else as far as my eyes can see. Veeru, sitting alone gazing at the sea, reminds me of a German painting (that I must have known when I was alive). *Wanderer above the Sea of Fog*. Except that in this case the wanderer is sitting on a beach, not standing over cliffs; the sea is real and made of dark waters, not fog; and the wanderer is wearing t-shirt and shorts, not coat and trousers.

The wanderer is wearing a t-shirt and shorts! I look closely. Yes, I have guessed right: the wanderer is shivering too as he gazes at the sea. It's windier now; though I can't feel the wind, I judge that from the fact that the waves are far stronger now.

Why is he sitting there in a t-shirt? The idiot! He must be feeling pretty cold! How long has he been sitting there?

I walk up to him. "How long have you been sitting here?"

He starts and turns his head. "You are back?" He is looking at my legs as I stand by him.

"Yes."

"I was worried," he says. "You took really long."

"I am sorry," I say looking at the sea. "I was surfing for some time and then I decided to wander a little."

"Above the sea?"

The words strike a chord. I look down. "Yes, above the sea."

He nods. "Won't you sit down?"

"*You* should stand up. Aren't you feeling cold? We should go."

"Yes, we should go," he says, but makes no effort to get up. "How did it feel to wander above the sea?"

I hesitate, then tell him. "Good. It was… spacious. I felt like a… a…"

"Bird?"

"Yes… that's the right word. Bird. I felt like a bird. Like a seagull."

"Yes, I can imagine. It must have been beautiful. Water as far as you can see, the strong winds bearing —"

"I can't feel the wind."

"You can't? But you just said it's cold?"

"I can't feel it. I guessed from the waves."

"You are pretty good at guessing. Aren't you?"

I ignore the mild sarcasm in the words. "Veeru, let's go please."

"Why? Why can't you sit with me here for a while?" He pauses. "Unless you want to wander some more?"

I sigh and sit down. "You are angry with me? Aren't you?"

"Angry? Why should I be angry?"

"I don't know. It seems you are."

"No, I am not angry. I am just sad. I wish I was wandering with you instead of sitting here and looking at the sea, waiting for you."

The grey, restless painting rises in my mind again. The wanderer. Are we both wanderers of different sorts?

"Why were you waiting for me?"

"Why was I waiting? You didn't come back for a long time! I was worried!"

"Worried?" I ask quietly. "Why… worried? What more can happen to me? I am a ghost, I am already dead! You should have slept. What was the point in coming here?"

"I don't know. I don't have an answer to that." He shakes his head. "I couldn't sleep. I was waiting in the room anyway. I thought waiting here would be better."

We are both silent for a while. Only the waves keep crashing.

"Don't wait for me anymore."

He doesn't say anything.

"Do you hear me?"

"Yes," he says softly after a few moments.

"Those who wander come back sometime, even if it's a long time. I won't. After a few days, I won't come back. Don't wait."

There is silence for a few seconds again. Then he says in an even voice: "Yes, you are right. One should be sensible. Not to wait is the sensible thing to do."

I can't make out his tone – if it's sincere or mocking. From what I know of him, I am suspicious it's the latter.

I feel wretched. I wish I could help my words, but I can't. It's the truth, however bitter: I won't come back. Even if I don't find freedom and get stuck here on earth, I won't come back. Whatever happens, I won't come back.

I am sure of that after today's talk with ma'am. I have already caused enough damage. I don't want to anymore.

"Let's go, Veeru," I say in an almost pleading tone.

"Let's sit out a bit. All this talk of wandering reminds me of a painting, you know."

My heart sinks. I spring up from my seat on the sands. I don't want to know what painting! "I have to go," I tell him in an urgent tone.

He looks up surprised. I notice he never looks into my eyes, still pretending he can't see me. "You have to? Why? What happened?"

"Nothing happened. I just want to go. It's too late. We have to get up and leave early."

"Yes, it *is* late, too late. Isn't it?" He sighs. "You go ahead. I will come soon."

I don't know what to do. I don't want to leave him, but given the mood he is in, it's likely he won't come at all if I don't go first. I decide to teleport behind a rock nearby and come back to push him again if he doesn't get up to go in fifteen minutes or so. That seems to be the best bet.

I do that: I teleport behind a large, mouldy rock and wait for time to pass. I have waited for five minutes when suddenly I feel uneasy. Something is wrong somewhere. What?

I look at Veeru. He still sits at the same place gazing at the sea. Nothing wrong there.

I look around and then I notice what has made me uneasy. About hundred metres to the left almost parallel to me, two men are looking towards Veeru and discussing something. They are having a heated discussion; though I don't get the language being spoken, I understand that one man wants to do something while the other man doesn't and keeps shaking his head. In a span of maybe a minute, the first man points at Veeru twice, and once he sweeps his right hand across the entire landscape.

I smell danger; it's not difficult to get the meaning of those potent gestures. What if the first man prevails? At once, I teleport next to Veeru. "Get up and come with me immediately!" I tell him in as urgent a voice as I can. I look back; the men are still arguing.

"You didn't go back?"

I ignore that and almost yell at him: "Just get up and come with me!"

His eyes widen. "What happened?"

"I will explain later. There's no time! Just get up and come!"

I don't want to explain the situation to avoid arousing in him the male instinct of facing the danger than fleeing when accompanied by a woman. That the woman in question is a ghost invisible to any man and so logically not the one in danger may not register with him as easily as it has with me.

"Okay," he says getting up with a frown on his face. I sigh with relief.

I look back again. Yes, it's as I have feared: the first man has prevailed. I see the men start to descend stealthily down the gentle slope. Once – I guess seeing Veeru get up – they even hide behind a big boulder among the many that strew the landscape.

"Let's go!" I almost scream.

Veeru looks back too. "What happened?" he asks puzzled. It seems he can't see the men yet.

"Just walk… *please*! I will tell you in the room."

He nods and we start walking. I look back; they are gaining on us.

"Faster! As fast as you can!"

Veeru shakes his head and tries to look back as well.

"Don't look back! Just walk!" I shout at him again. "*Please.*"

This time he does exactly what I have said. He bends his head down and walks. Soon, we are walking at an extremely rapid pace. I look back again. To my relief, the men are now falling behind. I keep looking back. After another minute or so, I see them stop, gaze at Veeru and talk with each other. After another couple of minutes, the second man starts retracing his steps and the first man follows him after hesitating for a few seconds.

Soon after, the men disappear from sight. Still I am not comfortable and we keep walking at the same brisk pace for the next twenty minutes till we reach the main beachfront. A small number of people are up even at this time of the night.

Veeru breaks the silence first. "Can we slow down now?"

I nod. "Yes, we can."

"Great! Can I now ask what—"

"There were two men following us."

"Two men?"

"Yes, two men. They saw you sitting alone near the creek and I think they wanted to rob you."

"I didn't see anyone!"

"I know. But I did."

"How do you know they wanted to rob me?"

"I was watching them."

"Watching them?" He is astonished. "But how? I thought you went back to the room."

I am caught. "I didn't," I confess.

"You didn't? Then where were you?"

"I had teleported behind a rock close to you. I thought in another fifteen minutes or so, I would again try to persuade you to return."

"Teleported to a rock…" He stops abruptly and turns. "So you were watching over me? What do you think I am?" he asks in a caustic tone. "A kid?"

I take the ghostly equivalent of a deep breath; I have to keep my temper under control. "I wasn't watching over you," I tell him. "I was waiting for you to change your mind about not coming back!" I pause. "And it was good I did that. You would be in danger if I hadn't."

"Thanks!" he says to that, sounding least thankful, and starts walking.

"You are welcome," I reply, sounding equally waspish. "And please don't stay up waiting for me in odd places at odd times. I don't want to be responsible if something happens to you."

On hearing that, he stops with a jerk and is about to say something, then closes his mouth. "Sure," he says after a brief pause, "I will keep that in mind," then walks on.

I walk after him, feeling horrible. I didn't want to be sarcastic. Why does he have to fight with me?

And then I realize what an unfair thing I have just told him. He has been helping me since yesterday, obviously taking responsibility for what happens to me. I, however, have just said I don't want to be responsible for what happens to him!

No, that's not what I meant. I do want to be responsible. I do. It's just that I *can't*… even if I want to. I have no time.

And the more he stays with me, the more danger he is in. I know that now. I discussed a lot with ma'am today. I wish I knew two days back all that she told me today; I would never have let Veeru come with me at all. I would have tried to find some other way. But she says she didn't know it herself.

And now it's too late. As ma'am conjectured, he may already be trapped. And the only way out for him is through me: by helping me find the oblivion, by succeeding in doing what we are doing, he can be free of me.

I can't leave him now even if I would like to. We are in this together. And I know I have to find the oblivion, anyhow. For his sake as well as mine. There is no other way to free him from me.

Friday, Goa

VEERU:

There was an unacknowledged distance between us the next morning. We almost kept quiet as I quickly got ready so we could leave by about eight-thirty. The plan was to visit the three hospitals, Asilo Mapusa, GMCH and Hospicio Margao, in reverse order of their distance from our hotel – we would go to Hospicio Margao first and then come back to visit Asilo Mapusa and GMCH. This would help us save time: we planned to cover the distance between our hotel and Margao between eight-thirty and ten am – a time when the hospitals were yet to open with regard to our purpose of checking emergency records.

I avoided looking at Maahi as I readied myself. She was no more a shimmering shape, but was as solid and substantial, as here and now, as any girl I had ever met. She wore a deep blue kurti patterned with clusters of thickly bordered white squares topped by a shining sky-blue dupatta and a yellow salwar underneath. On her feet were flats matching the colour of her kurti and on her wrists she had a silver coloured oval wristwatch and a pair of green bangles. Her hair was untied; and through the loose, lanky strands showed itself now and

139

then a pair of pearly tops. It was what she must have been wearing when she...

She looked achingly lovely, yet I wished she would become invisible to me again. At least when I couldn't see her, I didn't know what I wanted to hold in my arms, what I wanted to knock my nose against, what I wanted to caress and... now I knew.

There she was sitting on the chair and looking at me when I woke up (I barely managed to avoid her eyes), sitting on the bed and staring at the floor when I came out of the bathroom, leaning on the table with her back to me while I dressed, standing against the wall humming a song while I had my breakfast on the table, and sitting next to me while I drank coffee and as we both read (or in my case pretended to read) the newspaper kept between us (I turned the pages for both of us and she thanked me after every page).

She was so... there.

When I had reached the sixteenth page and my charade was about to end, I let my fingers brush against her hand as if by mistake. Hoping for I don't know what... maybe a miracle? But no such miracle happened and my fingers went through her hand as if they were made of air. I think she noticed what I did but she didn't say anything. By the time we got up to go, I felt pretty angry – I didn't know why or with whom.

I decided I didn't want to see her. It was much better when I couldn't. I didn't behave like a complete idiot, at least: trying to touch a ghost, and getting disappointed and angry when I couldn't. As for her, she wasn't the least bothered; while I hadn't read a line of the paper in the ten minutes I was pretending to read it. All I could do was gaze at her wrist and the back of her hand and her fingers and her lap and her feet...

"Veeru?"

I looked up at her lips. "Yes."

"Have you finished your coffee?"

I turned my head to look inside the cup. It was empty. "Yes."

"Shall we go then?"

I nodded. "Yes, let's go."

Yes, let's go. That's all I was, wasn't I? Just a guide to a wandering ghost, helping her find the final destination. I got up and walked out without a word.

While crossing the door, I had a thought. There was no one in the corridor, so when she followed me out, I told her: "You know, I just had an idea."

"What?"

"You remember Hospicio Margao?"

"Remember… Yes, of course I remember. We went there just yesterday."

I nodded. "Then why don't you teleport there directly and wait for me? Can you? Will save you a lot of trouble."

She was silent for a few moments. Then she said slowly: "Teleport there? Yes… I could. But why do you want that?"

"It's a long ride. It will be easier, less tiring for you."

She smiled thinly. "Physically, I don't get tired. Emotionally – when I am with you and talking to you, that's when I am least tired. There is nothing as tiring as being alone."

"I thought you liked wandering alone."

Once more, we had a short silence. She was looking at me; and I was looking at her neck. What was I doing?

Then she said: "Yes… that's true. I like wandering alone. I will go." And in a flash, before I could stop her, she was gone.

MAAHI:

He won't talk to me. He isn't even looking at me. What have I done?

At one point, I am so irked by his behaviour that I decide I am really going to make good my threat of teleporting into the bathroom the next time he goes to take a shower. That will show him not to ignore a ghost! In fact since he continues to pretend he can't see me, I think of calling his bluff by turning towards him all of a sudden while he dresses. Of course he would get shocked and yell at me, but then I would ask him how on earth does he know I have turned if he can't see me? I would kill two birds with one stone: have my revenge and call out his bluff, both.

Unfortunately by the time I make up my mind, he is already dressed. To break the ice between us, I then try singing. Knowing he likes my singing, I stand against the wall and hum while he has his breakfast. The effort, however, is quite lost on him; the complete attention he gives to his bread and butter and omelette and cheese makes me feel he was Bheem having his dinner in front of me, the disturbing Bakasur! I clench my teeth and devoutly wish I really was a man-eater like Bakasur; I would have gobbled him up with greater concentration!

After finishing his breakfast, he sits down to drink the coffee and read the newspaper; and I sit next to him pretending to read the same thing hoping he will break his silence. But I have hoped for too much; he stays quiet. Angry, every time he turns a page, I thank him in as formal a tone as I can manage despite reading not a word. But he doesn't notice and goes on reading. Men, I tell you!

Feeling disheartened, I am about to get up when I see his fingers brush against my hand as he turns a page. My heart leaps! Did that happen accidentally? Or was that on purpose?

I wish his thoughts jumped into my mind like they did before, and I knew what was in his mind; but that's not happening anymore and I don't know why. Since I am not sure, I pretend not to have noticed the incident.

I wonder what he was trying if he did that on purpose. Does he really think he would have touched me – a ghost?

No, that's not possible. It must have happened by chance.

And then I am sure that it happened by chance - he doesn't even want me to ride with him. As we come out of the room, he asks me to teleport to the hospital pretending that will be less tiring for me. When I say that it's when I am with him that I am least tired and being alone is what is really tiring, he tells me that he thought I liked wandering alone.

I feel hurt. I tell him angrily that yes, that's true: I like wandering alone and I will go. My eyes feel as if they are beginning to water and I teleport before he can see that.

VEERU:

I felt like banging my head against the wall after Maahi vanished before I could stop her. What the fuck was I doing? Acting like an asshole if anything!

Love is supposed to be uplifting and all, isn't it? Uplifting my foot! Ask me, it was the quickest way to start behaving like a total jerk!

In the last twelve hours, I had yelled at the girl I loved (or ghost I loved… whatever), behaved badly after she had actually helped me escape real danger, ignored her throughout the morning, and if all that was not enough, made it as plain as possible to her that her company was not welcome. And all this when she had done nothing but been good to me!

I went back into our room and sat down on the bed. I needed to do some deep introspection.

Best thing, I soon decided, was to call up Jerry. Not tell him everything, but just talk to him.

Jerry picked up my call within a ring. "Goa?" he asked even before I had said hello.

"Yes."

"Are you alive?"

I chuckled. Yes, calling up Jerry had been a good idea.

"I am talking, no?" I shot back.

He snorted. "Big deal. You could be a ghost and still talking. Someone told me even ghosts talk these days."

I laughed, but I wasn't giving in easily. "Your Rajnigandha ghost talked too, you told me. Remember… promises of no sex and all?"

"Forget my Rajnigandha ghost. How's your ghost doing?"

"Pretty good. I can even see her now."

"Really?" His voice couldn't get more disbelieving.

I swore on my mom.

"Don't bring Auntie in between!"

"Ok… Yes, you're right. Sorry I won't. But I am not kidding, man," I said. "I can really see her."

I was tempted to add that I had even fallen for Maahi. But I didn't want to give Jerry a heart attack this soon.

"Is she scary?"

"Not a chance! She's damn lovely!"

"What! Don't bullshit man!"

"I am not bullshitting. I swear!"

"Hmm…" He paused.

"You sure you are not being fooled? How did you start seeing her?"

"By concentrating like hell… Look Jerry, I'll tell you the whole story when I come back. Right now just take it from me that she's as genuine as you and me. And if I am being fooled… well, then whoever is fooling me will not have any trouble getting a Nobel Prize soon. So either way it's fine."

"Ok… I believe you dude," Jerry said sounding convinced. He paused, then asked again: "You having any luck finding the guy… You went to help her find some guy, right? Her lover or something… so she can find the oblivion? Did I get it right? It was the oblivion… right?"

"Yes, it was the oblivion." I paused. "No, no luck yet. We have to first discover who she herself is before we can find the guy. We are still trying to find out who she is."

"Shit! How do you plan to do that?"

"Searching for an accident on 21st July that involved a twenty-five… twenty-six year old girl. We will visit three major hospitals today."

"Hmm… best of luck."

"Thanks."

"There was some deadline too right?"

"Yup…" I sighed. "We have just seven days more."

"You doing good, man?"

"Huh?"

"You sound pretty stressed, you know."

"Yup… maybe. A little."

"For her? You're stressed for her?"

It was great relief unburdening myself to Jerry. "Yeah… Things seem pretty uncertain right now, and I don't know what to do."

"Hmm… How's *she* taking it?"

"Much better than me for sure."

Jerry chuckled. "You like her, don't you?"

I laughed. "Yes, man. A lot. I sometimes wish she was alive. I have a major crush on her by now."

Jerry caught my pulse in a jiffy. "She's that good? It's been just a day!"

"Yes, I know. She's really that good."

Jerry kept silent.

"Jerry—"

"Hold on, dude…Now I actually *don't* like this. She's a ghost you are saying… and you like her that much." His voice sounded worried.

Ok… reality check. Maybe I shouldn't have unburdened myself. At least, not this much.

"Hey… it's cool, man," I told him. "Don't worry. I like her because she's uh… very… nice."

"Nice?"

"Nice… yes… you know… she makes me laugh. I mean she makes me… I feel… *comfortable* with her."

And maybe that was the understatement of the century.

Jerry was not fooled so easily. "Sure. Good to know that she makes you… comfortable."

He added in a circumspect tone: "Just remember she's… dead. Dead like dead. Ghost. Not alive… and all that."

I laughed. "I know, man."

"Can you touch her?"

"Touch her? Of course not! How can I? She's a ghost!"

"Yeah… a ghost she is. And yet you told me you can hear her and even see her."

"That's different."

"Maybe. Good for you then. When are you coming back?"

"In eight days… hopefully."

"Which is after you guys find her lover and she's got her oblivion?"

"Yes."

"What if you guys don't find her lover and she doesn't find her… oblivion?"

I sighed. "I don't know, dude. Haven't thought about that yet."

"What will happen to her?"

"No idea. From what I know, she may get trapped here for a long time."

"Here means… on earth?"

"I guess. Where else?"

"You'll still be in touch?"

I was exasperated. "How do I know dude? I haven't thought about those things yet!"

Which was a lie of course. But I wasn't about to tell Jerry about my fight with Maahi. And her response about how long could she be trapped: theoretically, it could be till the universe ended, she had said.

Would we be in touch till the universe ended? I doubted.

And I remembered Maahi was waiting for me at Hospicio Margao. "Hey man! I have to go now," I told Jerry. "Maahi is waiting for me."

"She is?" he answered with a chuckle. "Tell me you are not shorting me, your best friend for a ghost?"

"No, dude!"

"Come on, dude. Tell me the truth." He laughed harder.

"I swear! She's waiting at a hospital."

"Okay, dude! Take care," he said giving in. "Help your ghost find her guy… and then please get back soon and preferably in one piece."

I smiled over the phone. "Yeah, will do… and will be in touch. I hope you are not pissed off with me?"

"Pissed off? Why? Because you shorted me?"

"No man! I sneaked off to this place without telling you."

He chuckled. "That's fine. I almost knew you would. Don't worry about that. Just take care of yourself."

I smiled once more. "Will do."

"And yes… one last thing…"

"What?"

"However *nice* she is, dude, don't fall in love with your ghost. Not a good idea." With that parting shot, my friend signed off.

I sighed. He was right. Except that it was too late for his warning. Then I called my parents for a quick chat (of course, without telling them where I was and what I was doing) before I started for the hospital at Margao.

MAAHI:

I teleport to the hospital lobby and then I walk away. When we were here yesterday, we had noticed a beautiful church on a nearby hillock; and after asking, we came to know the hillock was called Monte Hill and the church the Chapel of Our Lady of Mercy. I decide to visit the chapel till Veeru arrives.

Instead of teleporting, I walk to the chapel. I need help and I feel I should earn it before I ask for it.

I try not to think about what happened as I walk to the chapel; let me reserve my questions for the almighty. Fat chance. *Why does Veeru want to hurt me?* – I am wondering before I am out of the grounds of the hospital. And yet what's the point in asking God a question that I already know the answer to.

Actually, I know the answer to my question but I don't know what to do about it. I am hurt by Veeru's behaviour and I am tempted to dish it back to him. If he can ignore me and be formal, I can be twice as cool and formal.

But we don't have time to behave like a pair of quarrelling lovers. It's a luxury we don't have. No time for the innocent, small dramas of life. No time for the nearnesses and the distances, the fights and the make-ups. If I hurt him, I may not be able to make up with him ever.

And then there is another thing: I don't know, but I think hurting him back may bind him to me even more. You should hurt someone only when you have time to nurse them out of it; otherwise they get bound to you. I already wounded him without knowing it, and now he is trapped. I can't make things worse by responding to his anger. No matter how he behaves, I have to do my best to nurse him out of myself in the time that we have together, in the puny little thimbleful of time that we have. I can't allow silences between us, coolness between us; I can't allow a wall to come up. I have to go on drawing him back even if he pushes me away.

Last night, I slept again. I can sleep when I curl myself next to Veeru. How can I push him away when he is the only one whose closeness helps me sleep?

I slept and I had the dream again. The same one. A series of sounds and smells and images. A man calling me from far away. Golden hair. The roar of a truck. An elephant's leg smeared with white. Flowers. Bells. Children. Street. Traffic. Food, wine, glass. Blood. Moon. Sun. A huge golden ball. Incense. Top of a tree. The voice laughing.

"Don't be afraid, I am here."

Why do I have them? What do they mean? I haven't asked ma'am and I am also yet to ask Veeru; I will do that when he is more… approachable. I will ask them both together.

The chapel has come. It's a beautiful, white and cream chapel with one large door and two smaller ones. Just before entering the large door, I hesitate.

Are ghosts allowed inside chapels?

I sigh. Whom do I ask? No one can hear me, no one can answer me. I don't know what to do. I stand there for some time and then I decide to go away – I will pray from outside.

But just when I am turning back, I hear a gruff loud voice asking from inside: "Why are you standing at the door, my girl? Why don't you come in?"

VEERU:

We had decided we would meet in the lobby of the hospital, but Maahi wasn't there when I arrived. After waiting for about a quarter of an hour, I started looking around, but she was nowhere to be found. After searching for another twenty minutes, I gave up and came back to the lobby to wait.

I was worried now. Had she forgotten what this hospital looked like and had teleported to some other place? But if that was true – unless she had forgotten the hospital completely –

she would still have arrived here by teleporting a second time. Why hadn't she?

I decided to wait for another hour or so before heading back. I was sure that if nowhere else, Maahi could definitely teleport back to our hotel.

And then a scary thought entered my mind. Could it happen that even doing that wasn't possible for Maahi, that she had forgotten everything once again? That she didn't remember our hotel or even ma'am or me?

After that, time went by slower than a snail. Every minute I kept glancing at the lobby door. After some time, sitting at one place became impossible. So I came out and started pacing the grounds praying to God to let Maahi come back safely and swearing again and again that I will never let her go anywhere alone if that happened. I will never behave like a jerk again, never trouble her again. Just let her come back safely. Please.

My prayers were answered soon; I saw her enter the gates after another fifteen minutes or so had gone by. I was so... so relieved. I looked at my watch; it was going to be eleven.

Thanking god, I walked to meet her. Like I had promised, I was going to behave with her like a friend, and not like an unreasonable moron describing that inexcusable behaviour as love. In fact, I was going to behave exactly the way I was behaving when Asmi ma'am had left her in my care at the airport.

"Hey! What happened?" I asked her when I had reached her side. "You got lost?"

Maahi didn't say anything, but signalled something with her eyebrows.

"What?"

"Your phone!" she reminded me with words. "You are talking to thin air now."

"Oh… yes, thanks!" I said taking my cell out and started talking into it before I appeared like a lunatic to people around.

"So… what happened? Where were you?"

She revealed she had gone for a walk to a chapel nearby. We had found about this chapel situated on the top of a hill called the Monte Hill when we came here yesterday. She thought she had plenty of time till I came, so she had gone to say a brief prayer.

"Oh cool! How was it?"

"Pretty good." She paused. "I made a quite interesting discovery. That's what made me this late. Sorry for that."

"Interesting discovery?"

"Yes. In the chapel, I ran into another ghost. A very old ghost actually, a nobleman. My first one."

MAAHI:

When I look closely, the voice inviting me inside the chapel belongs to a handsome, bearded man – obviously a European judging by the fairness of his skin and the structure of his face – sitting alone in the pews in the third row from the back. From his peculiar accent, he probably belongs to southern Europe – Italy, Spain… one of those countries.

Wearing a plumed hat, he gazes at me in amusement while I am scared. How does he know I am here? How can he see me?

"Hello. Come inside, Miss," he prompts me again. "You are welcome here."

I ignore the invitation. Still not convinced, I stare at him, having half a mind to flee immediately.

"Are you a new ghost?"

Ghost? He knows I am ghost?

"I am a ghost too," he goes on. "Is this the first time someone is seeing and talking to you?"

I nod my head, not knowing what to say. He is partly right anyway. This is the first time I am talking to another ghost.

"Come on in then. Let's have a chat. It will do both of us good." He chuckles. "You look more frightened than a lost kitten, and it's a long time since I set my eyes upon a ghost as pretty as you." He stands up.

"Come on in, *minha mulher linda.*"

Instead of going inside, I stare at the dress he is wearing. I can't believe my eyes – it's so outlandish! He looks as if he is wearing the costume of a sea pirate. And what was that he said in the end? Was it some pirate language?

He grins at my wide stare. "Never seen a Portuguese man of war before, have you?" he asks snickering.

Have I? No, I can't remember that I have. But for some reason, I had the notion Portuguese men dressed like most other men in the world. Shirts and trousers, t-shirts and jeans… that kind of stuff.

"Portuguese men wear clothes like this?" I ask in a surprised voice as I enter the chapel finally. He seems genuine enough.

"They did… five hundred years ago."

"*Five hundred* years ago?" Now I can't believe my ears.

"I know." He laughs. "That's pretty old, isn't it? But I *am* pretty old though I don't look my age. I am Marquis of Fidalho, Dom Antonio Lopez D' Mello at your service, Miss. Landed in your country with Dom De Gama in 1524, murdered in 1529, and have been here a ghost a long time."

"Dom De Gama? You mean Vasco De Gama?"

"Yup… the same man. Dom De Gama. I was a close friend of his son Estevao."

I still have a doubt. "You say you are a Portuguese nobleman from the medieval times… right?" I ask him. "Marquis of… something?"

He laughs. "Yes… from the medieval times. Marquis of Fidalho. Quite the brutal barbarian."

I ignore his saucy retort. "Then how do you speak so good… umm… modern English?"

"That's not so difficult to answer. If you live five hundred years like me… with nothing much to do… you have the time to pick up half the languages in the world."

And yes, that's another thing I want to ask as it scares me – his five hundred years. "Why haven't you found the oblivion in such a long time?"

"All in good time, Miss," he answers smiling. "Why don't you come and sit with me first? I have plenty of interesting stories to tell."

Before I can answer that, a lady enters the chapel with her teenage daughter and they walk on to the front without giving us any notice. Not sure, I ask Mr D' Mello: "Are they ghosts too?"

"Oh no! They are very much alive. Don't worry, they can't see or hear us."

I sigh. "I know."

He laughs. "That sigh shows you are a new ghost." He beckons me once more to the leftmost end of the pew he is sitting on.

"Come here. We will sit and chat in peace. Haven't talked with a soul in days."

I hesitate. I have to get back to the hospital. Veeru must be on his way.

Mr D' Mello notices my hesitation. "What happened? Don't want to talk to a man as old as me?"

I shake my head. "No, it's not that. I have to get back to the hospital. I have a friend meeting me there at ten."

"What hospital? The one nearby? Hospicio Margao?"

I nod.

"Oh! Then you have enough time to spare for an old man, my pretty girl. It's only nine. I am sure you can teleport, can't you?"

I nod again. Yes, I guess I have time to spare. And despite his five hundred years, Mr D' Mello doesn't *look* old at all.

Suddenly, he frowns. "Wait a minute. You just said I am the first ghost you have talked to, didn't you?"

"Yes, you are the first one."

His frown deepens. "But… your friend…" He trails off.

"He is not a ghost."

His eyes widen. "Not a ghost? You already have a friend who is not a ghost? How long since you became a ghost?"

"Eight days."

"Eight days? Only eight days? Then you *must* chat with me, my girl!" he says. His voice bubbles with excitement and the feathers on his plumed hat flutter as he beckons me. "I have never met a ghost like you before. So lovely too!"

And even I have never met a ghost like you before, I am tempted to say. I smile, flattered at his enthusiasm, and join him at the end of the pew. Actually I myself am eager to talk to him, my first ghost, and on top of that he is a five hundred year-old Portuguese one.

Also, as Mr D' Mello has pointed out, I have plenty of time before Veeru comes. Because while I had a good reason not to teleport to this chapel and instead spend time in walking till here, there's none why I can't teleport back to the hospital around nine-fifty and get there before Veeru.

"So what brings you here to this chapel?" Mr Mello asks once we are sitting next to each other. "You lived somewhere close by when you were… err…?"

"Alive?" I shake my head. "Actually, I don't know. I am not sure where I lived. Probably in Bangalore."

He frowns. "You don't know where you lived?"

I shake my head again. "No, I don't. I have lost my memory. I think it was in an accident that I died and lost my memory."

"What?" he exclaims. "You are a real peculiar one, my girl." He keeps addressing me as 'my girl' and his eyebrows are knitted and his voice is incredulous.

"Don't mind my words, but I am astonished. First time I have come across a ghost who has lost her memory!"

I am tempted to say I *do* mind his words. I don't like the sound of them, I don't like them at all. I mean I am already a ghost, and in a way that is already peculiar. And so is being a trapped ghost not peculiar enough that I have to be doubly peculiar by being a peculiar trapped ghost?

I resist the temptation though. "You have met many ghosts?" I ask him instead.

"Plenty in my lifetime," he answers, "the ghost lifetime I mean. Remember I have lived for almost five hundred years."

"And you have never come across a ghost who had lost his or her memory?"

He shakes his head, the feathers fluttering again. "No. Not one."

"Did any of them die by accidents?"

He nods. "Oh yes, many. Many died by accidents. Horse accidents, car accidents, train accidents, plane accidents, fire accidents – I have come across all sorts. One woman I met some time back even said she was on the Titanic. She was a baroness, she claimed, the baroness of some place in Austria. The funny thing is," he winks and chuckles, "it was not long after the movie came out. But for sure she was no Kate Winslet as much as I am no Leonardo Caprio." He laughs heartily at his own joke.

I smile in return. Then he resumes his story in a far more subdued tone.

"Another child I met a year before was in that horrifying Mangalore plane crash. Poor girl was searching desperately for her parents, especially her mother. Still looking actually. She's too small to understand she'll never see them again. That… that's a real tragic story. I will tell it to you someday if we meet again. A third guy—" He stops abruptly.

"Wait a minute…"

That's the second time he has asked me to wait a minute.

"I am waiting," I say. I can be saucy too if I choose to.

"No… really. It's no joke. You said you died in an accident, didn't you?"

"I think so."

"But you're not sure?"

I knit my brows. "I… I'm quite sure. Why?"

"No, you are not! You hesitated just now! I saw it! Just for a fraction of a second, but I saw you hesitating."

"I'm quite sure," I repeat.

"It can't be an accident!" he exclaims again shaking his head. "Especially if you lost your memory too. It was a complete loss, wasn't it, Miss…" He stops to remember something. "Oh no! I don't even know your name," he says with dismay. "You don't remember that either, do you?"

"I have taken on a temporary one. You can call me, Maahi."

"Maaaa…heee," He pronounces it with emphasis and interest, the hat feathers fluttering again slightly. "Nice name."

He pauses. "Who gave it to you? You yourself… or your friend?"

I nod, "My friend. One of them."

His eyes widen again. "One of them? You have more?"

"I'll tell you later. You were telling me something important. You think I couldn't have died in an accident?"

"Oh yes, you couldn't!" he insists putting his hands in the pockets of his jacket. "That's quite impossible if you lost your memory completely. Where are your injuries if I may ask?" He looks me up from top to bottom. "You don't even have *one*!"

"Injuries? I should have injuries?"

"Of course! Accidents cause injuries, don't they?" he shoots back. "Especially if they were bad enough to kill you?" He pauses, his eyebrows arched. "And I am supposing as you have lost your memory completely, you couldn't have telemorphed yourself into this particularly lovely appearance?"

I frown. What was that he said? "I couldn't have done… *what*?"

"Telemorphed yourself… See, you don't even *know* what it is! But don't worry, that's nothing to worry about. Even I didn't know what telemorphing was till many days after I became a ghost."

"Yes, you are right. I don't know what this ... telemorphing thing is!" I pause after saying the strange, complicated word, trying hard not to show my anxiety. I haven't died in an accident? I mean... really? "But I'll be *glad* to know about it now," I add with emphasis.

"Hmm..." He gazes at me as seconds go by.

"Tell me... *please.*"

His brows knit again. "Who told you that you died in an accident?"

I look down at the sinuous carvings on the back of the pew in front of us. "Nobody told me," I confess. "We guessed. My friends and I... from the way I was talking when they found me. I was saying something about a crash and sound of waves. Incoherent stuff of course. So yes... it was a guess."

Could ma'am have guessed wrong, I wonder? I suddenly realize ma'am is not infallible. It's quite possible she could have guessed wrong.

"Hmm..." Mr. D' Mello nods his head. "What you should know is... ghosts almost never continue in the way they looked when they died. Almost always, death is not pretty to look at. Take me... you think this is the way I looked when I died? Of course not! For more than two weeks of my ghost-life, I was walking around in blood soaked clothes with a deep wound in my back and a long dagger embedded in that wound. That's how I died, murdered by one of my closest friends. And that's how I looked for many days, blood soaked and scary, before I ran into another ghost who told me how to telemorph myself into something less scary and more presentable to fellow ghosts. And so…" He pauses and points at himself with a grin. "I decided to look much better. A handsome and rakish and dashing nobleman instead of a terrified and terrifying murdered man. Ghosts can telemorph, you know."

I nod, trying to take it all in. So this is not the way he looked when he died. And what he wants me to understand is that the way I look right now is not the way I *could* look if I had died in an accident. I should have – as he's pointed out– injuries. Injuries bad enough to cause death.

"But the thing is…" he goes on. "To telemorph yourself into looking something better, you should have strong memories of your past. You can't telemorph yourself into just *anything*. We ghosts are not magicians from the Harry Potter world. You can telemorph yourself only into… yourself. Into what you *were* and importantly, what you *remember* you were at some point in time in the past.

"It's quite like *teleporting*," he explains further. "To teleport, you have to clearly remember the place where you want to go, isn't it? You can't just teleport anywhere."

I nod.

"And the way our memory helps us teleport, precisely in the same way it helps us telemorph too. We are in a way nothing but our memories. So if you vividly imagine yourself to be what you actually were sometime in the past, you become that. I can become this," he points at himself. "Because I vividly remember I was like this once upon a time."

I nod again. I think I understand him now.

"I can become a child too you know," he says.

"A child?"

"Yes… I mean I can become the way I looked when I was a child. Do you want to see?"

I nod politely. How can I tell him I am too scared right now to enjoy seeing anything! The only thing I can think of is: *It's quite probable I didn't die in an accident*!

Unaware of my anxiety, Mr D' Mello smiles, closes his eyes, and in the blink of an eye, there is a cute boy sitting next to me. "*Eu olho bom*?" the child asks me grinning.

"What?"

"Do I look good, Maahi?"

I grin back and nod my head. "Yes," I say bending down close to him and pinching his cheek.

"You look verrry cute."

In a flash, the boy turns back into the bearded man. "Aaaa…" I let out a yelp and pull back with a jerk as Marquis D' Mello breaks into peals of laughter. "Ha ha! Never pinch the cheek of a ghost," he tells me, still laughing.

"You never know what they might turn into. From smooth, chubby cheeks into rough, bearded ones."

I turn on him a mock glare. "That… wasn't… funny, sir."

"If you say so."

And then something else strikes me. "I just touched you," I exclaim at him. "I can *touch* you."

Really, I can't believe I just touched him. Despite the fact that I am ghost, I just touched another… ghost!

Marquis D' Mello smiles gently, as if an experienced teacher is smiling at the mistaken assumptions of a new, inexperienced student.

"You didn't touch me," he says shaking his head. "That wasn't exactly touch. You just *felt* you touched me."

What? I frown at him. "What's the difference?"

"In feelings… maybe none," he answers. "In actions… a lot. What you experienced is not the same as how we used the word touch when we were alive. You could touch me with a dagger if we were alive. Like my friend killed me with a dagger when we were alive. But now…" He shakes his head.

"You can't touch or kill me with a dagger now. In fact, nothing can touch me but a ghost like you. Everything else will go through me as if I was air or space. I am sure you must have experienced that." He pauses. "So can you really touch me? I don't know. I would rather say it was all in your mind… you just *felt* you touched me. Of course to our ghostly minds the feeling is exactly the same." He ends his explanation sounding like some scientist in a lab.

"But that is what matters… right?" I ask. "That it's the same feeling?"

"That's what matters? I don't know… maybe," he answers with a shrug. "It's a good way to look at things though. Positive thinking and all." He grins.

I shrug too and bring him back to my story – the story of how I died… or more importantly, *didn't*.

"So… you think I couldn't have died in an accident?"

"It's not about what I *think*, Maahi," he answers me a little crossly. "It's the truth, it's what happened. What other explanation is there? You haven't telemorphed ever, have you?"

I shake my head. "No."

"Yes, you haven't… because in any case you couldn't. You don't remember anything from your past. You don't have any memory," He pauses.

"So how come you are like this? Beautiful, flawless... without any sign, any mark that death ever touched you! Death is never so gentle, at least not to people who she leaves trapped. Forget accident. How come you look as if... as if you never died at all?"

I have no answer to that. I don't know enough, so I stay silent.

"Tell me about your friends," he says after many seconds have passed by. "You have many, don't you?"

"Not many. Two."

"*Two* living friends. That's still a big number for a ghost eight days old! Let me hear about them."

And so in short I tell him about Asmi ma'am and how she found and sheltered me in my pain; and about Veeru and how we found him and asked for his help; and then how Veeru and I started together on this journey to find Hrithik, the guy who I had loved when I was alive and who ma'am thinks is the key to the door barring my way to the oblivion. The Marquis listens attentively and nods from time to time as I tell him my story.

"You are in a lot of pain?" he asks when I have finished.

"Yes. But it's going down. Sometimes I don't even know it's there."

He nods. "I expected that. Even I was in a lot of pain just after I died. It was the shock of being betrayed by a close friend. He literally stabbed me in the back. But slowly the pain went away as I got lost in my new life. Happens to everyone who stays back on earth for a long enough time. It's like love, I guess. You move on sometime, no matter how attached or hurt you were."

"Are there a lot of ghosts in the world?" I ask.

"Depends on what you mean. Most of the people automatically find oblivion as soon as they die. As a percentage, very few souls are trapped. But many people die every day, so even that percentage is a big number. And yet…" he pauses for a second, "the world is a *lot* bigger place. So most of us ghosts are quite lonely most of the time and desperately wishing for the oblivion… as you know."

That reminds me. "Why didn't you find it?" I ask. "The oblivion I mean? It's been a long time."

He sighs. "Yes… it's been a long time. Five hundred years is a long time. And I don't know why I never…." He stops midway and smiles. "I guess because I never had an Asmi ma'am to help me." He smiles wider. "Or better a Veeru to give me company till I found it."

I smile too. "Yes. I guess I am lucky that way."

"Very lucky." He nods.

"Especially since nobody knows why we get trapped and how can we get out. Many theories exist, of course, as you can imagine. It's the favourite topic of discussion when two ghosts meet." He grins.

"How did you die? Why did you get trapped? How do you find the oblivion? Blah blah blah…"

He pauses.

"And yet I doubt anybody really knows. We just guess the answers that seem obvious because the real reasons may well be beyond us. It's like astrology than science. No universities and research departments exist in our ghost world, you know… or scientists for that matter. There is no methodical quest for the truth, just hearsay and speculation. And anyway why should anyone care for the truth when you can stumble upon the oblivion anytime, find your escape. Unlike me, most ghosts do stumble upon oblivion sooner or later – usually sooner. And then there is a bigger problem. Finding your escape is different from being trapped. At least you can get trapped ghosts to talk to about what happened to them, gather some evidence to form your theories from. Oblivion?" He shakes his head with lips upturned. "No one ever came back from the oblivion. No wonder it remains an even more mysterious territory than the question of what traps us here."

I nod, and then ask him the question I have been waiting to ask for a long time. "Have you really seen anyone find oblivion? I mean like… really *seen*?"

He nods. "Yes. Once."

Yeah! Manna from heaven! I gaze at him with big, expectant eyes.

He smiles. "Don't give me those big eyes Miss. I am telling you stuff anyway, am I not?"

I give him another silent toothy grin.

He goes on. "It was a long time back… in 1952. Sixty-one years ago to be precise." He pauses and remembers with faraway eyes. "I was with this Spanish woman. We had been together for eight years since 1944."

He pauses again. "Do you know anything about the Spanish Civil War?"

I shake my head.

He gives me a stern look. "Everyone should know about that war if they have any interest in the freedom of mankind, Miss!"

I purse my lips. Isn't it too late for me to interest myself in the freedom of mankind? I don't say that aloud though. Mr D'

Mello, far far older than me in ghost world, obviously doesn't share that pessimistic opinion.

He shrugs. "Let me tell you anyway. She was a Republican… my Olivia," His eyes mellow and his voice softens as he takes her name. "Olivia Fernandez. Almost her entire family died in the '37 bombing of Guernica. She herself survived, but not for long. She went to fight for the Republicans soon and was captured while fighting Franco's troops in Valencia in '38." He paused.

"And then the Nationalists tortured her to death in prison two months later… the bastards!"

"You loved her?"

"Loved her? I *adored* her. I…" He stops and sighs. "I had loved my wife too. But now that I look back, what I felt for Ines was nothing compared to what I felt for Olivia. Life with Ines was good… Olivia was…" He stops again and shakes his head. "…no comparison."

"How did you meet?"

"Like what it is often… serendipity. When Franco became the President after the Nationalists won in '39, she left Spain with many other Republican ghosts in disgust and crossed over to Portugal. My own country in her opinion was not much better under the fascist Salazar, but she was in Seville and Portugal was nearer. And then very soon France got occupied by the Nazis so she couldn't go there. Thank God for that. My apologies to the French people who died under the Nazis, but I wouldn't have met Olivia otherwise. Anyway, I had gone back to Portugal in '40. It was a time of war and great sorrow in the world, and as a Portuguese soldier, I felt it would be right if I was in my country in such troubled times. I mean even India is my own country now, but you know I felt…" He stops.

I nod my head. I can understand what he felt.

"Anyway, I was in Braganca when I met her, a town close to my birthplace. It's a town very close to the Spanish border on the north and in a way closest to France. Portugal happened to be full of trapped ghosts then, especially Spanish and French ones. The civil war in Spain had already claimed innumerable lives, both Nationalists and Republicans, and if that wasn't enough, Franco the victor was torturing and killing the Republicans right, left and centre. To the north, many people had perished in France too because of the World War. And then there were always the multitudes of Jews fleeing Germany and Europe, even as ghosts. Almost all had died violent deaths and seen their close relatives die the same way too and so many had got trapped. In a paradoxical way, it was one of the best times of my ghostly life. For the first time, I forgot there was something called loneliness. And I should be ashamed to admit it, but I did rue why I hadn't visited the place during the previous world war as well. There were so many of us running into each other, here and there, every day." He pauses. "Yes, the ghosts were unhappy and often in great pain, and often didn't even speak the same language, but not lonely." He shakes his head. "No, not lonely. Despite our pain, or more likely because of it, we met for big night-time parties and sang and prayed in chorus in whichever languages we knew for Allied victory in the World War and hoping that would help kick out the bastard Franco as well. Wine couldn't flow, but songs, jokes and laughter did." He pauses again. "I met Olivia at one such party in '44. The Allied forces had successfully invaded Normandy a couple of months back and were now pushing the Nazis back and she was ecstatic and ready to cross over to France so she could enjoy the sweet victories. That's how she had come up to Braganca from Lisbon. Well, we met, and then met again, and then again, and then again and again, and then finally left together for France two weeks later." He pauses.

"How did she find the oblivion?"

He grins. "Want me to come to the point, do you? Sorry…" he says grinning wider. "The topic of Olivia always gets me very chatty."

"It's okay… it happens," I tell him smiling. "And that's a great compliment to pay to someone you loved."

"To Olivia?"

I nod. "Ask any girl. If we are so chatty about something, we either love it or hate it."

"Talking of compliments," he says grabbing the word, "You know what?"

I raise my brows.

"Compliments…" He grins. "I remember there was this one time I was fishing for a compliment myself. I asked Olivia… I think it was in '51, a year before she… Well, we had been together for seven years and I asked her how she felt being with me. You know it's extremely rare ghosts stick together for that long a time. Things happen… usually one of you finds the oblivion or you split… Anyway, you know what the girl said?"

I shake my head.

"She said it was a miracle we were even together! She being a young liberal socialist worker and I an old, fossilized conservative nobleman! The rascal!" He looks up at the ceiling with fond remembrance in his eyes.

"She called me old and fossilized and conservative. I… and a conservative! Can you imagine such an insult? Have been forever a liberal democrat no matter how many beastly titles you hang around my noble neck!"

I just smile at his declarations; I don't have the heart to point out that liberal democracy didn't even exist when he was alive.

And so the Marquis goes on and on, about Olivia, and himself, and how being a born liberal he was from the beginning staunchly in favour of Goan and Indian independence, and then about the close and long-lasting friendship he had shared with Tristao De Braganca Cunha – the father of Goan Nationalism and one of the rare men the Marquis had come across who could talk to ghosts without fear… Wistfully, he talks and talks, about Olivia's fondness for dancing and Braganca Cunha's partiality for spicy food and his own love for travelling, especially over the blue waters and many more things. I don't have the heart to stop him. It seems he has found someone to talk to after a long time.

It goes on and on till I suddenly realize that the time must be way past ten and Veeru would have already reached the hospital and would be feeling very worried at not finding me.

"What time is it?" I force myself to interrupt the Marquis' reminiscences while he is telling me about a summer he spent roaming with Olivia near the Baikal Lake in Siberia where some guy called Trotsky, whom Olivia idolized, was exiled.

"Oh! I am so sorry!" he says with a stricken face, also realizing that I was going to be late. "It's almost quarter to eleven!"

I shrug. We can't do anything about that now. However, I must leave immediately.

"It's okay," I tell him. "I'll go if—"

He cuts me short. "It's not my fault you know… It's *your* fault!"

What? I am surprised at the unexpected and weird accusation.

"Miss…" he goes on with a stern glance. "Do you have any idea you have eyes that make people want to talk and talk and forget there is such a thing as time?"

Oh, that way! I smile at the compliment. It's beautiful. "No, I didn't. But I'll remember from now on."

"Yes, you must!"

Still, he doesn't let go of me and after apologizing once more, insists on letting him tell me about how Olivia found the oblivion. He swears he won't take more than five more minutes. I let him; five more minutes won't make a difference when I am already an hour late.

And then he tells me how it happened while he and Olivia were on another of their wanderings – in Brazil on the island of Ilhabela, about two hundred kilometres from Sao Paulo. Ilhabela was a beautiful place, he says. The name itself means in Portuguese 'a beautiful island'. Along with a group of Argentineans unaware of their presence, he and Olivia were relaxing on the Castelhanos beach on the eastern side of the island. It was a slightly chilly April evening and the Argentinean party lit a bonfire after the sun had gone down. Then it was time for food and drinks and everyone ate and drank and laughed, and once everyone was slightly drunk, a woman brought out a guitar, another man a violin and they played as a duo while two other women started singing with the rest joining in a chorus from time to time. Many songs were sung, including one of Marquis' favourites: *Besame Mucho* – kiss me a lot.

And then the man on the violin began playing solo, the rest of the group just listening to him. The old man was a marvellous player, and he played from the heart, completely lost in the sound of his own music. He played *Meditation* and *Salut D'amour* and *Elegie* and even one of Paganini's difficult *Caprices*.

"And then he played something I wish he had never played," the Marquis says softly. "I know I am being selfish but… Anyway, he did what he did. Played *Plaisir D'amour*, that old song of love and betrayal. He was playing the song like a virtuoso, and I was focused on him, and everything around me… the people, the beach, the mountains, the trees, the waves, the moon in the sky, the song floating on the breeze… everything… everything seemed so beautiful and full of love… And I was reminded of Olivia. My Olivia… Something made me turn around and look at Olivia."

He pauses.

"That expression on her face… I will never forget that expression on her face. She was… she was looking at the sky. It was as if she was opening herself up to the sky. I don't think anything else in the world existed for her, not even me. Just the music… and the sky. There was no white light or fairies or angels or any of that shit. It was just a call to the sky, a mute, intense call to the sky. Take me into yourself, take me into the infinity, take me into the oblivion.

"And then suddenly… she was gone. The music had ended too. It had taken her away with itself into the starry vastness.

"That's it. That was… oblivion. I don't know what did that song remind her of, what made her go along with it. She had never talked of it before. *Plaisir D'amour*. The pleasure of love." He laughs bitterly.

"Pleasure? It took my love from me."

We are silent as a child squeals with pleasure behind us and her mother tries to quieten her saying they are in church. He turns to look at them. "I have been quite alone since that day," he says sighing.

VEERU:

"According to the Marquis, I couldn't have died in an accident!" Maahi kept saying that again and again after she had returned from praying at the chapel. She was extremely worried about what the Portuguese ghost had told her, justifiably so, and we didn't know what to do. We thought of discussing the discovery with ma'am, but she wasn't picking up the phone.

"Are you sure he couldn't have been wrong?" I was talking to her directly after we had found a place to stand away from prying eyes. I was no more pretending I couldn't see her – the time for such foolishness was past – and even she was too agitated to notice the difference.

"No, it's doubtful he was wrong," she shook her head emphatically.

"He has been a ghost for five hundred years. He would know what he was talking about. Unless… unless he was lying about his five hundred years. But why would he do that?"

I shrugged. Yet, she was right. Why would he lie?

"And his clothes," she pointed out. "How could he be wearing those outlandish clothes unless he was genuinely from the sixteenth century?" She paused. "Of course if we want to keep doubting, we can always speculate he died while on the stage acting the part of a Portuguese nobleman!"

I nodded. She made sense; the clothes he wore made it very unlikely that the Marquis was lying.

And that was a scary thought to chew on. If Marquis was not wrong, that could mean only one thing: Maahi hadn't died in an accident!

Had we been chasing the wrong wild goose all this while?

MAAHI:

After about an hour of trying, ma'am finally picks up our call. "What happened?" she asks us, her voice anxious. We have called her six times in the past hour.

Veeru has already put the phone on speaker and I take the lead in the conversation this time. "I met an old Portuguese ghost," I tell her.

"Portuguese ghost?" Ma'am sounds tickled. "Where?"

"In a chapel close by. We are at the Margao hospital and there is a chapel close by at the top of Monte Hill. I had gone there to pray. I was wondering at the door whether ghosts were allowed inside or not when he saw me and called me in."

"Why wouldn't ghosts be allowed?" Ma'am laughs at the idea. "Anyway, he was Portuguese you were saying?"

"He definitely looked European and later I discovered he was Portuguese. He was also very old. Almost five hundred years."

"He told you that?"

"Yes. And from the clothes he wore, it looked that was the truth. The clothes were pretty ancient…."

"So what about this ancient Portuguese ghost? What happened for you to call—?"

"He told me I couldn't have died in an accident."

"What?" Ma'am sounds stunned.

I repeat what I have just told her.

There is silence for a few moments. Then ma'am says: "That's very worrying news. If that's true, I am sorry for guessing things wrong. But why does this Portuguese…" She stops.

"Did he tell you his name?"

I nod. "He said he was Marquis of Fida…" I stop and try to remember the rest, but I can't. "… something…"

"What?"

I skip the Marquis' full title so that I don't confuse ma'am. "Marquis Antonio… Lopez D' Mello… that was his name," I say limiting myself to what I remember exactly.

"Really? What a name!"

Ma'am's tone almost makes me smile despite the fact that I am very tense.

"Yes… quite a name," I say.

"He said he was a Portuguese nobleman and had come to India with Vasco Da Gama in the sixteenth century. He was a friend of Da Gama's son…" I stop and try to remember the son's name, but I have forgotten that too. "I forgot the name of the son… But yes, that's what he told me."

Ma'am replies, "The son's name is not important now. So why does this Antonio… Mello… that's the name, isn't it?"

"Yes."

"So why does Mr. Mello think you didn't die in an accident? Did he tell you that?"

"Yes. He said I had no injuries. If I died in an accident, I must have died of injuries. Those injuries should show on me. But I don't have even *one!*"

"Oh!" Ma'am's voice shows relief. "Is that all?"

"Yes. But isn't that worrying?"

"No, then it's not. Don't worry," ma'am tells us with a comforting laugh. "What he said is not true all the time."

Ma'am then explains to us why. She says that plenty of ghosts do go around in bodies they were wearing when they just died – bodies showing how they met with death – and look quite frightening as a result.

But many other ghosts are luckier. Rather, they have earned the right to look better. After dying, these second kind look what they looked at a special time - a time before their death when they had experienced an extremely powerful emotion that was more powerful than their fear of death. Those who were lucky enough to have experienced such a powerful emotion while they were alive – for example most mothers – were likely to find themselves after their death in a body that didn't bear the marks of death but rather carried the intensity and strength of that powerful emotion which had made them – in a manner of speaking – win over death.

"You know most trapped mothers look wonderful when compared to other ghosts," ma'am goes on. "And many fathers too. Add to that caring siblings and true lovers. Actually that holds true for anyone who has loved something or someone more than themselves, anyone who could have willingly died for what they loved. They all look wonderful. And you, Maahi…," ma'am tells me, "…you are one such lucky person, I am sure. So don't worry about your lack of injuries. That's something to be happy, and not worried about."

I experience some relief after hearing ma'am's explanation – am actually quite glad. And yet I can't help remain anxious. I mean lack of injuries may not mean I didn't die in an accident, but it also doesn't mean that I *did* die in one. Even now, we don't know anything concrete that clearly tells us *this* is how I died.

And then there is Marquis' comment on my loss of memory.

I talk to ma'am about that too. "Mr D' Mello also said I was a very peculiar ghost," I tell her. "He said never before he had met a ghost who had lost her memory."

"Hmm… that's strange."

"Have you met a ghost like that?"

"Of course I have. You are one!" ma'am exclaims. Then she softens.

"Yes… haven't met many… memory loss is not that common. Not even for those who are alive. But yes, there *are* a few ghosts who lose their memory." She pauses. "Look… you guys are in Margao hospital now, aren't you?"

"Yes."

"So why don't you first finish combing the three hospitals today? Then we can be almost sure Maahi didn't die in Goa and discuss in the evening what to do next? We—"

Veeru cuts her in between. "But ma'am…" he says, "… we have just seven more days. Every moment is precious. If Maahi didn't die in an accident, then—"

"But we don't *know* that yet Veeru," she tells him. "We are just guessing one way or the other… aren't we? I want you guys to first finish the task you went to Goa for before we discuss and change our action plan. Call that the whim of a professor, but to give a day to finish making sure Maahi didn't die in an accident in Goa is not really a waste of time. At least, we will know what definitely *didn't* happen."

And that is final.

VEERU:

I could understand why ma'am was insisting we finish searching the hospitals before we discussed anything else. It may be that we would return in the evening disappointed. But at least we would make sure that the Goa trip was indeed a wild goose chase before we started on another one.

Ma'am was right. While in Hospicio Margao and Asilo Mapusa, no one admitted in an emergency on the 21stof July matched Maahi's description, in GMCH we had a glimmer of hope: I was told that a young woman named Manasi Sharma had been admitted with her cousin after a bike accident on the twentieth and had died of head injuries in the hospital a day later, though her cousin had survived.

Sharma, while being a surname that is found in many parts of India, is also found in Bihar. So we were briefly happy. However, when I enquired further, we found Manasi was not from Bihar but from Raipur, the capital of Chhattisgarh, and had come down to Goa to visit her uncle who worked as a manager in one of the bauxite mines.

Still, we decided to go to Manasi's uncle's house; migration from Bihar to Chhattisgarh, two neighbouring states, was a possibility. We cooked up a story wherein I pretended to be a friend of Manasi come to Goa with former classmates from the Byron Bazaar Holy Cross school in Raipur (we gathered the necessary information from the internet).

To the uncle, a Mr Dinkar Sharma, I said that our group was on our way to Bambolim beach when one of the girls had met with a minor accident. Further inventions consisted of the girl falling down from her scooter and getting a deep cut on her arm; we going to the nearest hospital, GMCH, to get the wound stitched; we running into a nurse on duty who also happened to be from Raipur; some of us starting a chat with the nurse while the wound was cleaned up; and then the nurse telling us that coincidentally there was another girl from Raipur who was brought to the hospital after a bike accident about a week back. The nurse said the girl was brought in a much worse condition and unfortunately, had died the next day from head injuries.

I said to Mr Sharma that from what the nurse described, it seemed to me that the girl could be the Manasi I knew through common friends. Having seen her fit and fine not a couple of months ago, I was shocked. So I had got from the nurse Mr Sharma's address and had come down to see if it was indeed the Manasi I knew. I requested the old man if I could look at any photograph of Manasi to check if it was the same person.

I don't think I was very convincing, but Mr Sharma was a trusting person; in a few minutes, he had his daughter bring for me a photograph of Manasi posing with her uncle's family. While the photograph came, the two of us talked about the other person involved in the accident: Manasi's cousin who had escaped with minor cuts and a couple of fractures because he had been wearing a helmet.

The photograph came at the moment Mr Dinkar was describing the miraculous hand of divine providence that had saved his son. My heart beating like a sledgehammer, I took the snap from his daughter's hand and looked at it tilting it at the same time so Maahi, sitting on my right, could see it properly too.

Once our brief inspection was over, a tasty cup of tea made by Manasi's chachi followed. But I was far from enjoying it; unless people changed their appearance completely after they died, the subdued looking girl in the photograph I had just seen was definitely not Maahi.

What a strange place life had brought me to. I was unhappy that the dead girl in the picture was *not* the girl I loved.

MAAHI:

After an eventful day that for a short time makes me wonder if I am someone called Manasi Sharma from Raipur, my fellow ghost the Marquis is proved right and we return to our hotel empty-handed. While I should be disappointed, I am not; I have been expecting this. Rather I am looking forward to tonight's discussion with ma'am and Veeru.

I want to include the Marquis too but I have a feeling ma'am may not appreciate that. Anyway, inviting the Marquis is not possible. I have teleported twice to the Monte Hill Chapel and I haven't found him anywhere. God knows where he is.

After we finish dinner, rather after Veeru finishes his dinner, we call up ma'am at eight. Veeru has already messaged her about the day's events.

It's time to talk to them about my strange dreams.

VEERU:

Ma'am seemed surprised when Maahi told us that she had been able to sleep and dream the last night (I, not knowing enough, didn't know how to react).

"That's great news," ma'am said, but I felt her voice wasn't happy enough to match her words. There was something she was keeping back from us.

However, she was very interested in Maahi's dreams and asked her to describe them in detail. So Maahi told us about the waves (which meant ma'am wasn't wrong at least about Maahi dying close to the sea). Then a man calling her from far away in a language she didn't know though his voice sounded familiar (her lover?). Golden (blonde?) hair (belonging to the same lover?). The roar of a truck (something common, so there was nothing to be gained here). An elephant's leg decorated in intricate patterns with white (suggested a temple elephant?). A garland of flowers (tallied with the temple theory). Bells ringing (now I was sure it was a temple). Children laughing (could be anywhere). Glimpse of a street (again, could be anywhere). Cacophony of traffic (the same street? anywhere). Tables and chairs, smell of food, a bottle of red wine (together with the tables and chair and the smell of food, the bottle of wine suggested a restaurant). Glass broken on the floor (could be the same restaurant?). Wine and/or blood everywhere (this was inexplicable – maybe the colour of wine had suggested the colour of blood?). Moon… and sun? in the sky (the entire earth actually). A huge golden ball? in the sky (another inexplicable image). The smell of incense (back to the temple theory). Light streaming through the trees, top of a tree, and finally the voice of the same man laughing and saying "Don't be afraid, I am here" (again, these images could be from anywhere).

And then Maahi fell, fell and fell, till she woke up with a scream.

It was a strange dream as most dreams are. And since neither ma'am nor I had any knowledge of Freudian psychology, we tried our hand at interpreting it the ordinary way.

We started sequentially. The waves, all of us agreed, suggested that Maahi had died close to the sea. But the question remained that if death had not occurred through an accident – and there was a big 'if' here – then how had it occurred? And where?

Had the incident happened in Goa itself? Or was it in some other place also close to the sea?

After listening to Maahi's dream and knowing that she could teleport, I feared that this 'another place' could be absolutely anywhere in the world. Ma'am had found Maahi wandering in Bangalore; and if after her death Maahi could teleport to Bangalore from Goa, she could teleport to Bangalore from even Timbuktu. When combined with the fact that the guy in Maahi's dream had golden hair and spoke in a strange language, the inference was worrying.

For the time being, I kept my worry aside and went to the next image: the man calling her from far away in a language she didn't know. Since the voice sounded familiar, all of us agreed that the man was most likely Hrithik, the lover we were searching for, and that the golden hair and strange tongue suggested that he was from a foreign land.

The golden hair of Hrithik reminded me of a song: *chaandi jaisa rang hai tera, sone jaise baal* (your colour is of silver, your hair is of gold). And despite all my resolutions, I couldn't help feeling a sharp pang of pain and jealousy. My colour was brown and my hair was black. Maahi already had a much handsomer guy with the colour of silver and hair of gold.

The common interpretation of the rest of the dream was also fairly similar to my earlier interpretation. Similar except for the broken glass which ma'am said could be from the accident since the broken glass imagery was immediately followed by blood; and except for the huge golden ball in the sky which ma'am thought was significant since it was the only thing in the dream that was extraordinary. In fact, in ma'am's opinion the golden ball was so significant that she believed the door to understanding Maahi's dream lay through nowhere else but the ball.

However, even after a lot of thinking and brainstorming, we couldn't come up with even one reasonable interpretation of the golden ball in the sky. After guessing that possibly it was some sort of ride in a town fair or in an amusement park, we got stuck. I wish one of us wrote science fiction; maybe the task would have been easier then.

At last, around twelve, we ended the almost four-hour-long call after deciding to continue the discussion in the morning. I glanced at Maahi. She looked worn out and sad.

The night went by restlessly. Not able to sleep, I gazed at Maahi while pretending to sleep. She vanished soon after she thought I had slept, teleporting to God knows where. I wondered where she had gone to… maybe to surf on the sea again. Maybe she liked doing that when she was worried, unhappy. I twisted and turned till she came back about half an hour later, lay down beside me, and closed her eyes.

Feeling a little calm, I shut my eyes too and began thinking. We were in a fix again. What should we do next?

The next thing I knew, it was late in the morning.

Saturday, Goa

MAAHI:

It's very early in the morning, Veeru sleeps next to me, and I am thinking about what we discussed the night before as I ruffle his hair which I like doing immensely (though since I can't touch a single strand, I am not sure if I can call it that). Ma'am believes that the fleeting, disturbed image of the huge golden ball in the sky is the key to understanding my dream. If decoded, it should lead us to what we seek. To what I seek: to the facts of my death; to the answer to 'who am I'; and most importantly, to the identity of my lover – the man with the wavy, golden hair calling to me in a language I don't know.

And then, once I have found my golden haired Hrithik, I should find my way to the…

Oblivion reminds me of the Marquis. That old, old talkative Marquis. Where is he now? In the night, I teleported to the chapel once more in the hope of finding him, but he wasn't there. I wish I could find him and talk to him again.

I think about the Marquis' five hundred years on this earth, about his eight-year-old relationship with Olivia. I remember him saying they met in 1944, when the Allies were pushing the

Nazis out of France. I also remember that Olivia was killed in '38, six years before they met.

Olivia was trapped as a ghost for fourteen years then, from '38 to '52. That's also a long time… as long as the banishment given to Rama.

And she too must have been in great pain. Olivia – with her whole family bombed in front of her eyes and she herself tortured to death in a prison. It was a horrible death, followed by a fourteen-year-long yearning for escape. *When I will be free?* – she must have been thinking like me.

But then I remember it couldn't have been that bad – the Marquis was there to ease her pain later on. Maybe she was even happy with him. Maybe as happy as he was.

And yet…

I think about them both. She survived her fourteen years as a ghost, Marquis has survived his five hundred. Suddenly, I am not so afraid of being trapped. If Marquis and Olivia could bear being trapped for such long times, why can't I? I don't think I am such a delicate darling to not be able to bear what others can.

Which reminds me of another curious fact. It's about the man in my dreams. Even after knowing he is perhaps Hrithik, the lover I have been so desperately seeking, I don't want to find him as much as I should. I feel towards him just a mild curiosity now, nothing more.

My yearning for the oblivion has lessened too. I am almost comfortable where I am at present. Lying next to Veeru, ruffling his hair. Comfortable, when I should be worried to death since we are at a dead end and don't know what to do further.

What's happening? Is the man with the golden hair not the man I seek? Perhaps I have to see more than his golden hair and hear more than his voice to feel something more? Or is something else the matter?

I wish I could find the Marquis. I feel he would have the answer.

I teleport to the chapel again. But… no luck again.

VEERU:

The breakthrough happened with the call that came around ten o' clock, about an hour after we had had another round of conversation with ma'am and decided to return to Bangalore for the time being. It was a woman from the GMCH – an assistant to the chief clerk, she said. She had seen and heard me when Maahi and I had gone enquiring there yesterday; and after making up her mind to call me, she had taken my number from another clerk with whom I had left it so I could be informed if anything relevant turned up.

"I don't know if what I have to tell you will be of any importance," she began.

"Don't worry about that," I told her in an assuring voice, as much as I could manage with Maahi standing behind me. The speaker was on. "Any information is welcome, important or not."

"Anyway, you knowing about it can do no harm," she said as if convincing herself about that.

"It won't," I assured her again. "And if you want it to be so, I will guarantee what you tell me will not go beyond me."

"No, it's nothing like that. You can tell it to anyone else too."

"Can I know your name?"

"That's not important."

"Okay…" I trailed off.

She caught my signal. "Three days before you came, two persons, a man and a woman, had come asking for almost exactly the same information."

My heart started beating fast, "Same information? What do you mean?"

"Yes. Like you, they also asked if any unidentified woman, someone who looked as if she was in her mid-twenties, had been admitted to the hospital in the past week at any time. The girl's actual age I think was… twenty-six. I mean that's what I think they said."

I glanced at Maahi. Even her face was dripping with interest. Finally, we had run into something promising.

"Who were these people? Where had they come from?"

But we were not fated to be *that* lucky. "I am sorry, but we didn't take that sort of information from them," the woman said. "You see… nothing of that kind had happened in the past week… no unidentified young woman was admitted after the twentieth and they said it had to be after the twentieth… so we didn't take their details."

"But they may have—"

The woman forestalled me, "No, they didn't leave any name or number behind. I am sorry."

This was really disappointing. After such a promising beginning, even this lead seemed to be going nowhere.

God! Please help us!

"Didn't any—" I began.

I was interrupted. "But I do remember overhearing one thing," the woman said. "Goa wasn't the only place they were searching for the missing girl. I think they were headed for the east coast next."

"East coast?"

"Yes. They were talking about going to some place in Tamil Nadu near Chennai. One more thing. The woman who came looked Indian, but the man was a good looking Portuguese man."

My heart jumped up! "A Portuguese man?"

"Yes. The man was definitely a foreigner and they were speaking to each other in Portuguese. I know the language a bit. Learned it from my mother. It was actually strange because the man was dressed in awful clothes from like… long back. As if he was an actor in a play and had forgotten to take his costume off. He looked rather funny. If you—"

And then suddenly the call got disconnected.

MAAHI:

The call ends just when I can't believe my ears. A woman accompanied by a handsome Portuguese man in strange clothes asking about a missing young woman! Who else could the man be if not…

By why was the Marquis searching for me? How on earth was I related to him?

We hope for some time that the assistant clerk will call again, but she doesn't. When we call her back, we find that the number she called from is one of the landline numbers of GMCH and we are asked to dial the desired extension or wait for operator's assistance. That's when we realize that we know nothing about the caller except that she is an assistant clerk in GMCH – she had declined to give her name and we don't even have her number.

How do we find out more? It seems going back to GMCH is the only option.

We talk to ma'am again, and we reason that if the Marquis and the Indian woman had gone to GMCH looking for me (assuming it was me), then they would have searched in other hospitals as well. So there is a slight probability that someone in those hospitals would have information about them – got deliberately or even by chance – that could be of use to us.

Soon, like yesterday, we are back to our sortie of the hospitals.

VEERU:

It was a day full of mystery. I mean normally you would assume that a strangely dressed Portuguese man accompanied by an Indian lady going around hospitals asking for a missing girl would be noticed and remembered by some or other person in those places, especially if the incident had happened three days back.

Well… apparently not. Not in some twenty-five hospitals and nursing homes and clinics, big and small, we hurried through the day in trying to cover as much ground as possible. Towards the end of the day, we were rushing like maniacs, but all that effort came to naught. No one, absolutely no one, remembered having seen or heard of a Portuguese man or even an Indian woman asking for a missing girl in her twenties. The clerk at Asilo Mapusa who did remember me from yesterday said – her voice laced with pity – that I was the only such person. Maybe she thought I had gone mad.

Even at GMCH, we faced the same situation. No one remembered meeting those two persons; and not only that, no one even admitted to calling us in the morning.

It was as if the woman who had called us never existed. It was as if she was another… ghost?

MAAHI:

Suddenly it appears we are meeting too many ghosts. The woman who called us in the morning doesn't seem to exist. Nor do we – despite roaming in and around the Goan hospitals the whole day – find the strangely dressed Portuguese man and the Indian lady searching for a missing woman in her twenties.

By the time we come back in the evening, Veeru is tired and bewildered. I remembered he looked almost as worn out yesterday – after we failed to solve in the night the riddle of the golden ball. I hate to see him so stressed, but I don't know what to do. I have almost stopped caring about the oblivion and I am tempted to tell him that we should chuck it all and just return to Bangalore. What's the worst that can happen? I will be trapped right? And like the Marquis, forced to roam on the earth for hundred, two hundred, five hundred years… maybe a thousand years?

It's ok. Why not? I mean remembering the way the Marquis looked and talked, it doesn't seem so bad. Ok, maybe it will be bad, but why worry about those days now. I will take them as and when they come. And anyway, it's better than seeing Veeru so dejected and worn out all because of me and my damn oblivion.

Thinking like this, I feel like a desperado. Being trapped will be my adventure I feel. I will go anywhere, teleport anywhere. Free like the freeest bird! I am tempted to sing and dance and challenge the oblivion.

I won't pursue you oblivion, you'll have to find me; I will roam the earth till such time, careless and carefree.

Hurray! Let the trap do its worst.

Then I fall back to reality. I remember things are not so clear-cut anymore; I have complicated them myself, even if unknowingly. Veeru will not be free of me until I find the oblivion. If not for myself, I have to find it for his sake. He has his whole life ahead of him; and I am dead. I have to free him of me.

I sigh. No Marquis-like adventures for me. To the oblivion and beyond, that's the only way.

I force myself to bring my mind back on today's events. The mysterious call in the morning. Who made it? What was the caller's purpose?

To my mind, even if what the woman said on the phone never happened and no one was looking for a missing girl in the past few days, the caller wanted us to believe two things. One: the Marquis (and some other unknown woman) were somehow involved with my life… and maybe death. Two: they key to unlocking what had happened with me lies in some seaside town close to Chennai, and that's where the caller wants us to go.

But which town? How are we supposed to find it among the multitude of coastal towns near Chennai?

VEERU:

What Maahi said made sense. The call in the morning couldn't have been a prank call; the woman knew too much for that. Obviously, she had a purpose in calling us. And the purpose in Maahi's opinion was to let us know two things: that the Marquis (and a woman with him) were somehow part of Maahi's story, and also that the solution to this mystery lay in some coastal town near Chennai to which we should go.

I agreed with her; if you distilled the call to its essentials, those were the two pieces of information that remained. Still, the question was: which coastal town?

Once more, it was Maahi who suggested the way forward by connecting two things we knew. It seemed so simple after she made the connection that we kicked ourselves for not making the connection earlier.

Anyway, she asked me to go on Google and look for coastal towns near Chennai that had some sort of golden ball in the sky. She had a hunch we were going to find the mysterious ball of her dreams in one of those towns. If we were lucky that is.

The rest happened quickly. We made a snap list of sea-side towns close to Chennai. Starting from Pulicat with its famous lake and bird sanctuary, we skipped Chennai and moved over the map southwards. We noted down Mahabalipuram, Pondicherry, Cuddalore, Poompuhar, Karaikal, Tranquebar, Nagore, Nagappattinam and went till the almost right-angle turn in the coastline after Kodikkarai, the town with the historic Chola Lighthouse destroyed in the tsunami of 2004. We stopped with Kodikkarai as we were sure the towns beyond the kink in the coastline wouldn't be called close to Chennai by any stretch of imagination. Then putting the two key-words together – the town name and the phrase *golden ball*– we started our search on Google.

Well, Maahi was soon proved right, and ma'am too. And it turned out the caller of the morning had also pointed us in the right direction. Not long after, we struck gold in the form of the big ball in the sky.

MAAHI:

It's in Pondicherry! The golden ball is in Pondicherry!

And then in hindsight, suddenly it seems obvious it had to be so. Yes, if not Goa, where else but Pondicherry!

So I had died and (lived?) in the town of Aurobindo, Pi and Richard Parker? But of course! I guess that's how I know the little Tamil I know.

The man with the golden hair also makes sense now. Pondicherry is full of foreigners, especially the French. Was the language that Mr Hrithik spoke in my dreams French? No, it wasn't. I am sure of that. I know that much of French. In fact, it sounded more like English.

Anyway, Veeru and I are ecstatic. We feel like full-blown detectives, especially since it took us a little time to uncover the mystery once we started our search on the net.

At first, we were misled; disappointment hit us in the very beginning. Pulicat was the first town we searched; and coincidentally, some people had built near the lake in Pulicat a huge temple – apparently for mankind's spiritual awakening – and put a golden ball in its centre. So when we put 'Pulicat' and 'golden ball' in Google bar and searched, it led us to the wrong golden ball.

As we looked at the image, Veeru asked me if that's what I had seen in my dream, but I was sure it couldn't be so. What I had seen was not some small golden thing in the middle of a large room, but a gigantic sphere framed against the sky. By now I had seen it thrice, so I was pretty sure what I had seen.

A little disheartened, we moved on to Mahabalipuram. But the small, historical town famous for its Shore Temple had nothing to offer us in connection with a golden ball. Which was not bad; even if we didn't find what we looked for, at least we weren't misled.

Next on the list was Pondicherry; and the very first result on the page was a link from a travel site beginning with the words 'Matrimandir: very beautiful golden ball'. A cursory glance through the other results on the page mentioning phrases like 'large golden ball' and 'giant golden ball' and 'huge golden ball' told me that perhaps we had found what we were looking for. I mean what I had seen was definitely a very big ball.

But having been bitten once, I asked Veeru to go to the 'Images' pages before I said anything. The page loaded with multiple images of Matrimandir, and one glance at the first result told me that indeed we had found what we were looking for.

It was the same, giant golden ball in the sky I had seen in my dreams.

VEERU:

It was funny to see people looking for God in huge showy temples and shiny golden balls, large or small. Was it just a coincidence that out of the very first three towns we searched, in two of them people had turned God into a golden ball and were worshipping it? And to think we were guessing the ball was probably some sort of giant ride in an amusement park!

I was reminded of a famous Urdu couplet... I think by Khusrau or Ghalib... or Kabir?... well someone.

Let me drink wine inside the mosque O holy man, or show me a place where God isn't there.

You would think ten thousand years of civilization would have already taught us human beings such a simple thing. I guess not. Amazing godmen in our country and their still more amazing followers continued to be mesmerized by pomp and show and the shine of the yellow metal.

I glanced at Maahi. She looked so happy and radiant. We had unlocked her dream. Now oblivion was perhaps just steps away. Perhaps even tomorrow. We would find who she was; then find her guy, the man with the golden hair, the lover she was yearning to meet. And then she would...

With a piercing stab of pain I realized what had just been a vague possibility till now, an uncertain event of the future, had suddenly come much closer. Much much closer.

She would really go away. Five days. Or less...

And I have to be happy. She wants me to be happy.

Naazo andaaz se kehte hain ki jeena hoga.

I purse my lips. Ok, at least I can look happy, I *will* look happy... till she is here.

MAAHI:

Immediately after I have rushed through about fifty images of Matrimandir taken from all angles and made doubly sure that it is indeed the golden ball of my dreams, we call ma'am.

"We have found it!" Veeru bursts out the moment ma'am comes on line and says hello.

Ma'am doesn't need to be told what he is talking about. "Where?"

"In Pondicherry. It's some temple in Pondicherry. Matrimandir, Auroville."

"Auroville? I think I have heard of the place."

"Yes, I too have heard about it somewhere," Veeru says.

"So it's a temple in Pondicherry?" Ma'am replies to Veeru chuckling. "Not some ride in an amusement park?" The amusement park ride was Veeru's idea to begin with.

Veeru laughs. "No."

"Is there a flight to Chennai tonight?"

"We don't know. We haven't checked yet."

"When will you?"

I smile. Ma'am is back to her pure, natural bullying.

"We are doing it right now," I cut in before Ma'am can bully him further.

"Ok… I am holding."

While Ma'am holds the phone, Veeru checks a travel website for flights to Chennai. But we find there is none left so late in the evening; it's almost eight-fifteen.

"There is no flight to Chennai tonight," I inform ma'am half-yelling into the phone lying on the table.

"Bangalore then?"

"Bangalore? Why Bangalore?" Veeru asks. Even I have the same question.

"If you guys can come here," Ma'am explains, "I will arrange a cab to Pondicherry directly from the airport. The driver is pretty good and fast and he will take you to the town in about five and a half hours. You'll be there early morning. Even if you reach Chennai tomorrow by a morning flight, it will take you at least four hours to get to Pondicherry from the airport. Add the flight time… and the time taken is almost the same. But you will reach much earlier if you go via Bangalore."

We nod in agreement. Ma'am's idea has solid logic and we check for flights to Bangalore. Luck is with us tonight; there is a flight at ten-twenty. But it takes at least an hour and a quarter from here to the airport; we will miss the flight unless we are out on the road in the next ten minutes!

VEERU:

Maahi commented on our way to the airport that we didn't need to worry; lady luck was with us tonight. She was right. We managed to get to the airport just in time and were the last two souls to board the flight.

This time Maahi and I were on the aisle side, and no pretty young girl with a musical name occupied the window seat. Instead, it was filled by a stout, white-haired gentleman attired in white shirt, white trousers *and* white shoes! White from top to bottom! I had to give it to Maahi – she managed to attract interesting looking people even if not always young and pretty!

This time I made her sit next to the white gentleman as payment for the Ghazal filled morning. Uncharacteristically, she obeyed me without a word.

The flight was a quiet one. None of us talked, not even Maahi. We landed in Bangalore about quarter past eleven and found our cab arranged by ma'am and driven by Mr Doddamani. We were on our way to Pondicherry by quarter to twelve.

MAAHI:

We are quiet in the flight. I don't feel like talking. And even Veeru stays silent except once in the beginning when he makes me sit next to the man in white. He says it's revenge for making him sit next to Ghazal when we had come. I nod and accept my punishment.

Reminded of Ghazal, I think about her. Where would she be now? She had told Veeru she would be in Goa with friends till Sunday evening. So I guess in Goa still. Holidaying, happy. With still one more day to go. With still some time….

And more even when she is back to Bangalore. There is no need to hurry; for her, Goa will come again. And maybe again. And again. She has a lifetime to spend. Her end is not near.

My end is. And I don't want to go. I just want to know who I am. And that's it.

Not that I am afraid of oblivion, not anymore after Marquis told me what it is like. It sounded beautiful… peaceful…But I don't want it immediately. I want some more time on earth. Some more time to holiday, some more time to be happy. Some more time with ma'am, Marquis… Veeru…

Do people still find oblivion when they don't want it? Or am I the first ghost who is asking this question, the first ghost who doesn't want the oblivion?

And yet, I remember, I am the reason Veeru didn't call Ghazal. I look at Veeru without turning my head. He is reclining on his seat, his eyes closed. Perhaps sleeping. Taking time to rest.

He has time, like Ghazal. He *is* like Ghazal. They have a long life ahead of them. I am the odd one out.

And he may not call Ghazal unless I am gone. I sigh. I guess sometimes, *especially when you are the odd one out*, what you want doesn't matter.

VEERU:

Without acting on the phone, it was imprudent to talk to Maahi inside the cab we were riding to Pondicherry. Unless we wanted to scare Mr Doddamani out of his wits, especially since it was the middle of the night. It might lead to Mr. Mani asking his crazy passenger who talked to himself to get out mid-way.

So Maahi signalled to me that she was going to try to sleep and I should do the same.

I nodded, closed my eyes and tried to go to sleep.

But despite trying for a long time, I couldn't sleep. How can you sleep when the girl you love… You can't become normal just because you want to. Instead of sleeping, I kept seeing Maahi the way she had looked when I had first seen her fully two days ago.

The shimmering her.

The shimmering deep blue kurti with white squares. The shimmering light blue dupatta that lay over the kurti with the shimmering salwar below. The shimmering untied hair from which peeked the pearly tops that shimmered the most. Even the bangles on her hand shimmered.

She had looked like someone I know… I don't know who but she was so lovely, and I just wanted to… I couldn't sleep.

I opened my eyes and turned to look at her… she was not there!

I sat up with a jerk, drawing the attention of Mr Doddamani in the rear-view mirror. Where was she?

Had she teleported somewhere again? How could she? How would she know where were we going to stay in Pondicherry? We had not decided that yet. And anyway, forget the hotel, how would she teleport even to Pondicherry when she hadn't see the town even once? That was impossible for her. Had she forgotten she couldn't teleport to a place unless she had seen it and remembered it well?

The crazy girl! What could I do?

Then I had an idea. To test it, I flung my head back to rest against the seat; and then, as if I was singing a song, I called out

Maahi's name loudly in a sing-song voice putting it to the tune of an old song called 'Julie, I love you' though I also chickened enough to substitute the words 'where are you' for the words 'I love you'.

I was right. Immediately from the top of the car came Maahi's voice: "Veeru, I am up here!"

I *knew* it. That's where she would be. She loved the strong wind and the openness. I loved them too and wanted to go up there and sit with the girl I loved since we had so little time. But I don't think Mr Doddamani or even Maahi would have taken kindly to that. I had to continue sitting down here like a sane human being. You know, sanity is so rotten sometimes.

While I was cursing the sane world that forced you to conform to unnecessary rules and confined you to comfortable but passionless, bloodless boxes, Mr Mani suddenly piped up from the front: "Can you really see her?"

What? I almost jumped up. What was he talking about? I could see… *who*?

"See whom?"

"Maahi Avaru."

"What? How do you—"

"She's your dead wife, isn't she?" Mr Mani replied nodding with full confidence as if he had a perfect idea of what he was talking about.

My dead *wife*? What was he saying? And how did he know even that much? I was about to protest when Mr Mani went on: "Asmita Avaru told me the story of you guys. Very sad."

Hmm… I refrained from protesting. So ma'am had told him some sad story about me and Maahi in which Maahi was my dead wife! Why?

"What did Asmita Avaru tell you?"

"Don't be angry, I understand that—"

"I am not angry. I just want to know."

"Asmita Avaru told me not to get anxious if I see you talking to yourself. She said you had special powers that helped you see and talk to your dead wife. Then she also told me the story of how... err... the sad story of how... err... your—"

I completed his sentence. "How Maahi Avaru died?"

"Yes... so sad. I am so sorry."

"Thanks."

So that's how he knew. I was relieved. And I was thankful to ma'am for having the foresight to cook up such a story and tell Mr Doddamani. Now I could talk to Maahi as much as I wanted, without Mr Mani getting the heebie-jeebies.

Mr Mani was in the mood to talk too. "You loved her a lot?" Obviously, meeting a man who could talk to his dead wife and their story had got him interested.

I decided to pretend along. Sleep was anyway out of question and I had a growing desire to know what exactly ma'am had told him.

I nodded. "Yes, a lot." And that wasn't a lie.

"She was very lovely, wasn't she?"

"Yes... very," which wasn't a lie either.

"Ma'am said you were very young when you got married."

Hmm... the time for lying had finally come. And I didn't mind lying to cook up nice stories. Especially a story of me and Maahi in love? That wouldn't be too far from the truth also. At least, from my side. Rather you could call it wishful thinking.

"Yes, very young. She was seventeen, I was nineteen. We ran away from home to get married."

Wish I had really met Maahi when she was seventeen. I would be… sixteen. No, that was too young. A little later maybe. Maybe when she was twenty and I was nineteen. Or twenty-one, twenty…

I sighed. It was as wishful as it could get. When in reality I would be with Maahi for what five… six… seven days?

"Did you ever go back to your parents?"

"Yes… after two years. Once we were adults. They were happy to have us back."

Thankfully, Mr. Mani didn't ask what we did to survive in those two years. I would have had to invent things one can successfully do at nineteen and I don't think there are many!

"Any kids?"

"No… Before that she…" I stopped.

Mr Mani nodded. "Asmita Avaru told me. It was in a bike accident, wasn't it?"

So that's what ma'am had told him.

"Yes, it was because of me. My fault. I—"

Mr Mani cut me short before I could explain my imaginary fault. "Don't blame yourself. These things happen. They are nobody's fault."

I sighed. Yes, they are nobody's fault. "And yet she's gone." Or at least, will go very soon, maybe even tomorrow.

"You can really see her?"

I nodded.

"How?"

Maybe Mr Mani was expecting to hear that some godman or spiritual guru had helped me. I had to disappoint him. Godmen and gurus could help no one, except fool the gullible.

"I don't know. I can just do that." I paused. "Or maybe I hallucinate. Who knows?"

Mr Mani shook his head vigorously. "Don't talk like that. These are special powers, don't insult them like that. Or they may go away. They have come to you because you loved Maahi Avaru so much. You must respect them and thank God for giving them to you."

I nodded. I was certainly thankful to God that I could see Maahi.

"You are seeing her right now?"

I shook my head. "Right now she is sitting on the top of the car."

I cocked my head and listened carefully. Yes, it was what I had thought. Maahi was also singing. *Jab chali thandi hawa.* "She's singing. She loves the open air."

Mr Mani nodded with a big smile. I smiled too. He was definitely a romantic.

"You want to talk to my wife?" I asked him. I had an idea – to have some fun, tease Maahi a bit, maybe even tell her 'I love you' without getting boxed on my ears for that indiscretion. I wanted to do that before she went away.

"I can call her down," I added.

Mr Mani nodded spiritedly once more. "You can do that? Will she talk to me?"

I nodded back and told him yes, I could do that. He won't be able to hear Maahi, but I'll relay to him what she was saying.

"That'll be wonderful! Thank you so much! I have never talked to a ghost before!"

"But you'll also have to do one thing for me," I went on.

"What?"

"When she comes down, ask me to say 'I love you' to her and ask her to say 'I love you' to me. We have been fighting a little. Help us make up."

Mr Mani became even more excited. "Oh sure! I would love to do that."

After fixing my small set-up with Mr Mani, I yelled for Maahi asking her to come down.

"Why?" she yelled back from the top. "It's great up here. The wind is lovely. And don't yell like that," she went on. "Mr Doddamani will think you are mad."

"It's okay," I yelled again. "Mr Mani wants to chat with you."

"What?" This time her voice was surprised.

"Mr. Mani knows about you and wants to chat with you," I repeated.

She wasn't convinced. "Is this some kind of joke? Don't joke! And don't yell anymore! We will get into trouble!"

"I am not joking! Come down and see for yourself!"

In a second, Maahi was sitting next to me looking at me with eyebrows that were knitted and eyes that were not pleased. I became a little nervous. Ghost or not, she could be scary when angry.

"Is this some kind of joke?" she repeated. "And please pretend to talk into the phone. It can be dangerous to scare people in the middle of the night."

It was difficult to miss the irony of that last statement. Despite the nervousness, I broke into a grin.

Perplexed, she frowned some more. "Why are you grinning?"

Without answering her, I turned towards Mr Mani. "Mr Mani," I said, "Maahi Avaru doesn't believe me that you know about her. So can you tell her what Asmita Avaru told you about the two of us?"

"Maahi Avaru can hear me?" Mr Mani asked back, and gave Maahi a visible shock.

"Yes, go ahead. She can hear you even if you can't hear her."

"Maahi Avaru," Mr Mani began addressing an astonished Maahi. "Asmita Avaru told me the whole story of two of you so that I don't get bothered if Veerupakshya Avaru talked to you in the middle of the journey."

And then he went on narrating the short fictitious story that ma'am had told him – of our intense love, our brief togetherness, the sudden tragedy that fell on us in the form of Maahi's death in a bike accident, and then the final miracle that helped us still be together by helping me see and talk to the ghost of my wife. Maahi's face was worth watching by the time Mr Mani finished his narration under my expert prompting.

"So you see, Mr Mani knows that you are my wife and that I can see you and talk to you," I added in the end for extra effect. "We need not worry about him."

"Yes, don't worry about me," Mr Mani agreed with me. "I am so happy to see you two. So much love… Asmita Avaru said that's why you two can see and talk to each other."

Maahi stared at me blankly, as if at a loss for words. And Mr Mani kept glancing back, as if expecting some answer.

After about a minute, Mr. Mani asked me: "What did Maahi Avaru say?"

I raised my eyebrows at Maahi. Still, she kept silent. So soundlessly and with a pleading face, I asked her to say something. Maahi relented after a few seconds: "Tell him I am glad to meet him."

I turned to Mr Mani. "Maahi Avaru says she's glad to meet you."

"I am glad to meet her too," Mr Mani replied happily. "And you are so lucky to have each other."

"Yes, we are." I joined him in a toast to me and Maahi's non-existent relationship.

"Do you have small fights still?" Mr Mani went on in a significant tone.

I caught his cue. "Sometimes," I said, inviting an astonished look from Maahi. I shrugged. That was partly true anyway.

"That's okay. If wives and husbands don't fight, who will?" Mr Mani threw in a pearl of wisdom.

I nodded briskly as if in agreement while trying hard to control my laughter. "That's what I keep telling Maahi. Husband and wife do fight now and then."

"Are you fighting now?"

"A little."

Maahi watched the conversation with a totally puzzled face.

"Tell her you love her. Then everything will be fine."

"Say I love you?"

"Yes. You should say 'I love you' often." He twisted his body and threw a swift look where Maahi was sitting. "Shouldn't he Maahi Avaru?"

With a wide grin, I too turned to Maahi. "Should I? Right now?"

"Of course," Mr Mani answered me. "Right now. Life is short, isn't it? Why wait?"

Yes, why wait? But I *was* waiting for this moment. I wished I could hold Maahi's hand when I said the words. This was the first and maybe the last time I would say them. Maybe never again. But…

"I love you," I told her.

MAAHI:

"I love you too."

I realize with shock that the words have slipped out of my mouth. I am scared. This shouldn't be happening. This is wrong, dangerous.

I see Veeru's face. He is not acting. He means the words. And perhaps I mean them…

Suddenly, I am furious at Veeru. Why is he making me fight my feelings so much? Why is he making it so difficult? I don't want to hurt him.

"I love you," he repeats, with the same teasing smile on his face, pretending we are husband and wife. But his eyes are not teasing.

Then he turns to Mr Mani. "She's not replying Mr. Mani. She's still angry with me. What do I do?"

"What do you call her out of love? At home? I mean what's her pet name?"

"Dark Chocolaty. She's my dark chocolaty," he says bringing his eyes back on me. "I love you my dark chocolaty. Do you love me too?"

"Veeru! We—"

"Say you love me."

"Veeru—"

"No, first say you love me."

I am already bitter and that's the last straw. I blow up.

VEERU:

It was a sleepless night after Maahi went up to the roof again and didn't come down. Despite the anger and the intense pain, I didn't want to make a scene before Mr Mani, so I kept quiet. Realizing something had gone wrong, Mr Mani also stopped his small talk and went back to driving in silence. I leaned back on the seat and watched the night go by.

We reached our hotel on Calvay Street at about six-thirty in the morning.

MAAHI:

I lie down and count the stars in the sky. I cry without tears. I want to go down and say sorry, but I don't. I won't. Distances are better. I almost said "I love you". He said that too. We are both trapped.

I don't know how he will be free. He won't get his freedom if I don't get mine. And I don't know if I will find the oblivion before the rest of the days are over. I think I won't. I don't know what will happen then, what waits for me after that.

Just that I am sure I will not stay near Veeru. No. Distances are better. He loves me, and I…

Will I become a lonely wanderer? Will there be unending days of solitude, of loneliness? Like the Marquis said? Like his unending yearning for Olivia, will I be yearning for Veeru? I am back to square one. Back to unquenchable yearning. The pain inside has returned. I don't want it. What do I want? Why am I like a pendulum? The time when I am in pain – I don't want it. The time when I will be without pain – I don't want that even more.

I am angry, very angry. Yet, with whom? I don't know. No one I guess. No... with the sky. I am angry with the sky. I am angry with the moon. I am angry with the stars. They have so much time. They just look down and what do they do... pity us? Couldn't they lend us some time? I know I won't get any answer. They are the unmoved rich, I am begging from the unmoved rich. What am I blabbering?

I am tired. I want to go and lie down next to Veeru. I want to snuggle against him. I want to...

I can't. I have to keep him at a distance. I am afraid of dragging him into the loneliness waiting for me. I am afraid I have done that already.

Sunday, Pondicherry

VEERU:

Silence had returned between us. Maahi walked into the hotel without looking at me. I walked in a few minutes later after paying Mr Mani and listening to his assurance that things will become fine very soon; I should just keep trying to make up with my wife. I nodded. He was a good man.

I found Maahi standing next to the reception staring at the floor. My heart felt like lead. My head too. *Look up!* I wanted to yell at her. And I felt a rush of violence. I wanted to grab Maahi by her shoulders and force her to look at me. Hold her tight till she did that. Why was she untouchable? Why was she so... free? I felt helpless. Look at me! I wanted to hold her against me, bind her to me. See her, feel her struggle. I wouldn't let her go. My teeth clenched. Let her struggle. She would be helpless too. I wanted to make her helpless. Make her feel what I felt.

But she was so... unheld. So untouchable. So... free. She wouldn't look at me and I couldn't do a thing.

The receptionist greeted me with a smile. I smiled back at him when I actually wanted to throw the paperweight into the wall behind him. Smash the bloody clock to pieces. Rip time apart with my hands. Stop it. It shouldn't exist.

We walked to the stairs silently. We climbed the stairs silently. We walked through the corridor to our room silently. We walked into the room and I put my things in their places silently. Silently and unlooked. I sat on the chair, put my heavy head into my hands, closed my eyes, and tried to calm myself.

That's when I heard her voice after a long time. "You must be very tired." I jerked up and glanced behind. She was standing behind me looking down. "I think you should sleep."

She paused. "Sleep."

She put her hand on my head. I didn't feel anything. Or did I?

"Sleep", she whispered again.

Her eyes were soothing, so soothing. My eyes already heavy, drooped. Everything around me slowly faded.

MAAHI:

For the first time, I use my power of hypnosis. Ma'am had told me about it when I teleported to her place last time; she said the voices of some ghosts had hypnotic powers. Mine had too. She suggested I could use it to stop Veeru from falling for me.

I didn't quite like the idea then. It didn't feel right – to do something like that.

But today, I decided to use it. Veeru needed sleep, and he wouldn't sleep in the state he was in. So I made him sleep.

I have to take care not to make a habit of using that power. Perhaps I wouldn't stay long enough to make anything into a habit.

As Veeru sleeps, I lie down beside him and as usual, ruffle his hair. After sometime, I drift off myself. I dream again. But the dream I have this time is not a series of images. It's just one image, one sound. Repetitive. The man with the golden hair keeps calling me in his strange language.

VEERU:

When I woke up, it was almost one in the afternoon. I sat up with a jerk. I had wasted half a day of precious time!

Maahi sat on the chair looking at me. She was smiling.

Smiling? While I was sleeping? I was astonished. "Why didn't you wake me up?" I yelled at her.

Yes, why hadn't she woken me up? And when did I sleep anyway? The last I remembered, I was on the chair wanting to fight with her!

"It's okay. Take your time. We will—"

"Take my time!" I was incredulous. Had she gone nuts? "Today's Sunday, we have four days left... *four*! And half the day is gone. How can I take my time?"

She shrugged. "I know, but no point arguing. You needed that sleep. Get ready and we will leave."

I got ready in record time and rushed downstairs while Maahi ambled behind me as if we had all the time in the world. Once we had reached the small lobby, finding it empty, I made a gesture at her asking what the matter was.

"What?"

"Why aren't we hurrying?"

She ignored my question. "You should have something to eat before we go."

I was exasperated. "We don't have time, Maahi!"

In reply, she just smiled and said flirtatiously: "Veeru, won't you join me for a sandwich? And a coffee?"

MAAHI:

I made a resolution of keeping my distance from Veeru, but I can't keep it for long. When he gets up from his sleep anxious and guilty for having slept too much, he looks so cute that I can't help smiling at him.

Immediately, I get yelled at for not having woken him earlier. He then gets ready with the speed of a bullet train, rushes downstairs, and when I join him in the lobby, I find him exasperated at my slowness in coming down.

"Why aren't we hurrying?" he asks me.

Why indeed? I don't want to explain it to him just then, but partly it's because I don't feel like rushing anymore. I want the oblivion, but I don't want it enough to hurry.

And partly, it's also because of the dream I just had. My dreams, I feel, are not random; I feel they have a purpose of their own. As if they are living beings, telling me at certain chosen moments what I need to know to move forward in my search.

They wanted me to leave Goa and come to Pondicherry. And today they have shown me nothing else but the golden haired man calling to me. The sign can't be clearer. Rather than searching for my identity, I think they want us to search for the golden haired man.

I haven't told this to Veeru. But today while he searches in the hospitals for a girl of twenty-six, I will ask him to also enquire for the golden haired man.

So I am in no hurry. I have a hunch we will find our golden haired man soon.

Yet, I am worried about something else. I am afraid my heart knows what my dreams don't. I am afraid nothing is going to change with our finding the golden haired man. I have stopped thinking of him as Hrithik.

My Hrithik is right here, with me, while I have been searching for him all over the country. Isn't he? He is standing next to me, his shoulder is against mine.

I am with my Hrithik for a very short time – whatever happens, whether I stay or whether I go. I decide I won't have distances in that short time.

I will ask him for a coffee.

VEERU:

Why do girls like to drive you crazy?

A few hours before, she wouldn't even talk to me. Now, with a teasing smile, she was asking me to coffee!

What happened while I was sleeping, I ask you? And despite my protests that we didn't have time, I was dragged for lunch with the threat that if she didn't smell some lunch soon, she would eat me instead, she was a ghost so hungry.

Eat me? If only…

I didn't say that aloud though. I was with a hungry ghost.

MAAHI:

After I have bullied Veeru into having lunch, we come out on the street and find Mr Doddamani waiting for us. He says since he is familiar with Pondicherry, ma'am has asked him to stay back in the city and take us wherever we need to go. Apparently, one of the main hospitals of Pondicherry, PIMS, is quite far off from the city centre where our hotel is; and it would ease our travel if we have a fixed vehicle to move around. Since Veeru has also received a message from ma'am telling him the same thing, we thank Mr Mani for waiting for us and set out with him for the nearest hospital that provides emergency services: a Nallam Clinic situated on Easwaran Kovil Street, about half a kilometre from our hotel.

As we get into the car – and this time I choose to sit inside it – I hear Mr Mani whispering to Veeru asking if I am still angry with him, or have we made up.

"Made up," Veeru whispers back.

Mr Mani grins and gives him a thumbs up. "Where is she? On the top?"

"No, right next to me. And she can hear you."

Mr Mani deflates and quickly takes his place on the driver's seat, but I can see in the rear view mirror that he is still grinning widely. I grin too.

For another afternoon, I am Veeru's ghostly wife. His Dark Chocolaty.

I don't mind.

VEERU:

"I think we should also ask her for the golden haired man," Maahi told me when the nurse on duty in Nallam Clinic had given a negative answer to our question about a pretty girl in her mid-twenties being admitted to clinic on the 21st of July. And that was after being asked to give a description of the girl, I had described Maahi in detail to the nurse.

"Don't show off, Mr Veerupakshya," Maahi, giggling, had interrupted me in between as I looked at her and described her top to bottom to the nurse.

"She is pretty," Maahi went on, "but I am not sure if nurses fall for prodigious memories of other dead girls."

She giggled some more. "Besides am I not your wife, even if dead? You should be ashamed of trying to impress another woman in my presence! I can still haunt you, dear husband."

Though I had to try hard to stifle a grin, I didn't say anything; replying to my 'dead wife' was difficult in the situation. However, I did follow Maahi's advice and asked the nurse about the golden haired man.

But doing that was no help. Nallam Clinic on the 21st of July, or even on the 20th, 22nd and 23rd, had received on its beds neither a pretty girl, nor any man with golden hair.

From Nallam Clinic we went to Aum Hospital in Muthialpet, then south to East Coast Hospital in Moolakulam, and after that, west to AG Padmavathi Hospital in Victoria Nagar. And finally, to end the day, we travelled a few kilometres north to the well-known JIPMER in Gorimedu. But place after place we drew a blank. Neither Maahi nor the golden haired man was to be found anywhere.

The disappointing results were worrying me again. Maahi, on the other hand, didn't seem to care a bit. Her confidence in her dreams was astonishing. "Don't worry," she told me with a comforting smile. "I am sure we will find the man soon."

I didn't have the heart to tell her I wasn't so sure. And the most peculiar thing was that Maahi had started talking about the golden haired man, her Hrithik, as if he was just another guy we knew. As if there was nothing special about him. She didn't seem to be in any particular hurry to find him either!

Though I was surprised, I didn't mind.

MAAHI:

We are back in the hotel and sitting side by side. Why do I feel this is my last night with Veeru? Somehow, I am sure of that.

I am filled with intense pain at the thought of never seeing him again. Him – the guy who helped me make it through the night. I want him now, wish I could be with him. Touch him.

We couldn't touch. Listen and see, but not touch.

I feel it's the supreme gift of God. To touch and be touched. God gave life to man by touching him, isn't it? Gave us the most precious of all things: time.

I want to be touched by my black haired Hrithik. He has also given me his time. I want to lie down by his side, fold him in my arms and kiss him. Be with him.

I make him sit next to me and ask him about him. In the three days we are together, I realize we have been so occupied with my problem that we have never talked about him. Through obstinate questioning, I learn about his family: his father who is a doctor in Ujjain, his mother who is a housewife but runs a small business of homemade jam, jellies, pickles and spices, his elder sister who is many years older to him and is also a doctor and married to another doctor from Kolkata, his five-year-old niece who likes to stay up late and sing and dance in the middle of the night driving her overworked parents crazy, his younger brother who is studying to be a doctor too – a dentist. I ask him how come he is the only sibling who is not a doctor; and he nods and says with a grin that yes, it was certainly a matter of debate in his family – his mother wanted him to be a doctor. But thankfully his father, despite being a doctor himself, took his side saying that there were already enough doctors in the family as it was; Veeru could do what he wanted. He confesses botany was the subject he hated most till they made him go through something called engineering drawing in engineering college.

"Nothing could be worse than that," he says shaking his head. "I actually like biology now, even if not botany," he goes on. "Especially to know how the brain functions. It's… it's fascinating."

The enthusiasm in his voice is obvious.

"You can still become a doctor," I tell him. "A doctor of brains?"

"Neuroscience?"

He shakes his head. "I have already done my research. Takes too many years. And I read somewhere there are not enough jobs in the field either."

"You are not doing a job even now," I point out.

He shakes his head again. "That's different. That's a choice, not a compulsion. I can get a job anytime, I just choose not to. It's a totally different feeling from not having a choice at all. That would be painful."

I nod. I know that feeling quite well. Choicelessness. I want to sit next to Veeru and talk to him and know more about him, so much more. Know about him for days and months and years. But I don't have a choice either.

I have to find the oblivion, or stay a lonely ghost.

After we go off to sleep, I have the same dream again. The golden haired man keeps calling me. His voice is much louder now as if he has come very near. I know he waits for me on the other side of the night and I don't want to go.

VEERU:

Did she have to find the oblivion? I could be wrong, but I had the feeling Maahi was quite happy with me; and if not for her dreams, she rarely remembered her golden haired Hrithik.

It was almost as if we were on a travel date, Maahi and I. First Goa, then Pondicherry. Four days of dating, and somewhere in between I had fallen for her. Did she like me too? I felt so. I wished it was so.

I remembered my bet with Jerry that had led to me designing marryAghost.com and laughed at myself. Life plays twisted jokes on you, doesn't it? *I date dead people.* It was to take Jerry's case that I had made the website, and the whole thing had come true for me instead. Worse: I desperately wanted to date a dead girl while she… while I wasn't sure what she wanted.

Well, it wasn't so bad. At least in the eyes of Mr Mani, Maahi was my 'dead wife'. In his eyes I was married to a ghost even if I hadn't married a ghost like our site promised.

Maahi was unusually inquisitive in the evening after we were back from our unsuccessful sortie of the hospitals. After telling me not to worry, asserting that finding Hrithik was maybe a day or two away, she began questioning me about my family and my life.

I answered the questions reluctantly. Not because I didn't want to answer them. No, it was just the opposite; I wanted to keep talking to her. Tell her those things and so much more.

What bothered me was the way she started it and went about it. All of a sudden. And persistently.

As if she was in a hurry. As if there was a deadline and she had to complete the task by then. As if we were nearing the… end?

Monday, Pondicherry

MAAHI:

It's morning. After I have spent my usual half an hour trying to ruffle Veeru's hair, I plant a ghostly kiss on his forehead and go for a walk to a temple that we were told yesterday is near Francois Martin Street about half a kilometre away. If it's my last day on earth...

Following the directions Veeru was given yesterday, I walk straight from the hotel crossing Kasim St. and Netaji Subhash St. till I hit Rue Francois Martin at the corner of Aurobindo Ashrama. I turn right and walk past the small hospital and the art gallery to the crossing of Rue Law De Lauristor when I discover I have come slightly ahead of the temple. So I take another right turn into De Lauristor St. and within a minute come to a second crossing where Lauristor St. meets Manakula Vinayagar St.– the street named after the temple itself. I turn left into Vinayagar St. and a walk of another twenty-five metres brings me to the Manakula Vinayagar temple. It's a temple of Ganesha. I bow to the God who is almost like a child.

The early morning prayers are going on and there is a lot of activity. Bells are ringing inside the temple. Children (many of them escorted by their parents) dressed in different school uniforms are milling and running around and yelling and laughing and crying on the street outside the temple. Garlands of flowers of many kinds are being sold on the pavement. The air is filled with multiple aromas, especially those of jasmine and rose.

As I stand looking at the energetic, sometimes joyous, sometime cranky children, I suddenly realize I am standing on the street of my dreams. So many things I dreamt of are here: garlands of flowers, ringing bells, laughing children, the street. Yes, I am sure of it – it's the same street. I have been here before.

The only thing missing is the elephant with its legs decorated in intricate patterns. Perhaps the animal is taking rest today.

It makes sense. Ganesha is after all our elephant god. There is likely to be an elephant of the temple as it is in many temples of the south.

Just when I am about to enter the temple, I think I have caught a glimpse of the Marquis in the street. Surprised, I turn hastily when I see the man who is wearing strange European clothes (a combination of a frilly white shirt and an equally frilly black trousers which though less medieval than the dress the Marquis wore in the church is still a strange sight in 21st century Pondicherry) turn too and start walking swiftly among the crowd towards Nehru St.

I spring after him. Though I can only see his back, I am quite sure it's the Marquis: the man is of similar height, similar build and is wearing similar, strange clothes. And though I can't see his feet among the crowd, he seems to be gliding than walking.

The Marquis is going too fast for me. Has he seen me? I can't understand. He must not have seen me. Otherwise why is he almost running away?

In the heat of the moment, I even forget I can teleport. I keep walking after him, going faster and faster till I am almost gliding. I can't go any faster; going through people seems rude and horrible and I have to continuously stop and duck to avoid them as they can't see me.

In desperation, I start yelling after the Marquis. I yell as loudly and shrilly as I can; but he takes no notice of my voice, reaches the corner of Nehru St., turns right, and disappears from my sight.

I am also there barely seconds after him, but when I turn right into Nehru Street, there is no one of his kind to be seen as far as my eyes can see, which is pretty far. The street is dotted with ordinary people going about their daily routine; a few of them are milling around a restaurant at the corner of Netaji Subhash St. for their cup of morning coffee and breakfast. Otherwise the street is relatively empty because the crowd coming from the temple is mostly turning left and going the other way towards Francois Martin Street. I search among the people standing near the restaurant but there is no sign of the Marquis or anyone else that looks remotely like the man I was chasing seconds ago. Walking the length of Nehru St. till it crosses Netaji Subhash St. about hundred metres ahead, I look closely inside the three shops including the restaurant that are open at this early hour, but I am met with the same result: no Marquis.

Confused, disappointed and upset, I retrace my steps to the temple. I am bubbling with questions. Was it the Marquis? Why did he disappear? Why do I seem to run into him only near places of worship? If not the Marquis, whom did I just see? Only a living person wouldn't have heard my yells they were so loud and shrill, but if I saw a living person, how could he glide or disappear from the street within seconds? Aren't only ghosts like us capable of doing that by teleporting?

I don't get any of the answers in the time I slowly walk back to the temple. The puja is still going on. Bells are still ringing. Children are still yelling and running and laughing and crying. The garlands are still being sold. But my mind has lost its momentary peace.

What happened? Who was he? Why there are so many mysterious men in my life?

I am angry at fate. At least on this day, maybe my last on this earth, it could have given me peace. Is that wishing for too much? I am tired of all that's happening, I am confused. I want to go back to Veeru. I want to rest in his arms. I want to…

I realize I am in front of the temple. In front of Ganesha. I can seek his refuge too. I enter the temple and close my eyes. *Ganesha sharanam sharanam Ganesha*, I chant. I want your protection, help me. I tell him I am tired. I don't know what life is, what death is. I don't know why I am here, I don't know where I need to go, I don't know what's the meaning of all this. I am just a small, ignorant soul. I know I can't have life or love… Veeru… but I beg for peace. I want to rest now, just rest. Help me.

And then I also pray for freedom for Veeru. To let him be free of me after I am gone. Happy. Help him find someone like Ghazal.

Give me peace, I request Ganesha once again, just peace. I am ready for the oblivion, ready to disappear.

Veeru is still sleeping when I get back. I let him sleep late after he drowsily switches off the alarm when it rings. I lie down next to him and ruffle his hair while he sleeps.

When he gets up, he gets ready once more in a rush (though without yelling at me this time). He grins at me while he dresses, saying ruefully that he is late as usual. I try to smile back as my eyes burn.

Then he asks me out for coffee. I nod. Yes to a last coffee together. A stab of pain rips my breast. We should have had more cups of coffee, I should have asked him earlier.

But I lie to him when he asks me what happened and why I look troubled. I tell him I am worried because of what I dreamt in the night – I tell him I dreamt that we failed to find the golden haired man and I got trapped. I tell him I fear I may have been overconfident about finding the man. What if we don't succeed?

My words make him sad. He promises me that he will do anything and everything in the remaining days to find for me the golden haired man, that I will find the oblivion if there is anything good he's done in his life. He will not let me get trapped.

I feel like crying inside, but I nod and say thanks to him. How do I tell him I don't care much for the oblivion, and even less for the golden haired man? I can't tell him. I can't draw him any nearer.

I let him hurry me to the car. Why delay the inevitable?

VEERU:

Maahi was staring at me acutely when I woke up late after I switched off the alarm in my sleep. She was also unusually subdued as I hurried to get ready. The uneasiness and the sense of dread that had enveloped me last night returned with double the force – she knew something that I didn't, something that was troubling her. What?

To cheer her up, I made jokes on me being late again. And then while going downstairs, I asked her for coffee in the way she had asked me yesterday: with a flirtatious smile. Though she nodded and came, I couldn't get her to smile.

I didn't know what to do. I didn't want to take her to the hospitals. What was troubling her? Let's just take a day off, I wanted to tell her. Let's go waste some time. Don't go right now. Stay with me for a while. Sit by my side. *Yunhi pehlu mein baithe raho, aaj jaane ki zidd na karo...*

I may have been wrong, but since yesterday my heart was telling me that she also wanted to stay with me, that she was not so keen on find Mr Hrithik anymore. Or maybe it was just my wishful selfish thinking.

"What happened?" I finally gathered the courage to ask her when my breakfast was about to finish. The restaurant was nearly empty. "You look troubled since I woke up."

She opened her mouth to say something, then decided not to.

"You don't think I should know?" I asked her again, deciding if even this didn't make her open up, I will stop my questions.

It didn't come to that. "I had a bad dream last night," she told me.

"Bad dream?"

She hesitated a bit. "I dreamt we couldn't find the golden haired man," she said after a few seconds. "I dreamt I have got trapped and am roaming around like Marquis."

She paused. "Maybe I was overconfident about finding him. I am scared now. What if that dream..." She trailed off.

So that's what she was troubled about. I swallowed. We are good at wishing our castles, aren't we? Wishing our walls and gates and stairs and rooms and towers and turrets till a few words are enough to blow them away into thin air like wisps of smoke. And I was dreaming she had stopped thinking about her golden haired Hrithik. I laughed inside. Castles... how swift are we at making them, and how swiftly do they vanish

I looked at her, at the unhappy face. What is worse? The pain of knowing you will lose the one you love, or the pain of seeing them in a lot of pain... pining for someone else. I could see she was intensely unhappy – though she was also trying hard not to show her pain, though she was trying to smile and be normal despite it.

I felt horrible. How selfishly could I behave? She was in so much pain and all I was bothered about was if she had stopped thinking about Hrithik. It was agony – to be torn between the selfishness of wanting her to stay and knowing the pain that it would cause her. To be torn between promise, duty... and love? Could I call it love? Love? Wanting her to stay when she was in pain was not...

I hardened myself. I don't know what kind of person I was, but I had that much sense of right and wrong. Wanting someone without caring for them was not love by a far cry. I swallowed again and dragged a smile on to my face. I had made a promise; I should see it to the end.

No matter how, I would get her out of this pain.

MAAHI:

Pondicherry Institute of Medical Sciences is the second hospital we are visiting today. As we get on the ECR road after returning without any luck from another hospital in Lawspet, I feel I have been here, at this place, on this road, before. Actually,

I have felt like that continuously in the last two days – that I have been here before. But today as we travel on the ECR, the feeling is stronger.

I ask Veeru if I can go on the top of the car. I want to do that again – to feel the wind, to look at sun, to look at the sea. I want to lie in their arms, I want to fold them in mine. I may never see them again.

I want to kiss Veeru once. Taste love once, the pleasure of it. My own *Plaisir d Amour*. And then I want to disappear in it.

VEERU:

The reaction in PIMS, when we asked our usual question about the golden haired man, was diametrically opposite to the reactions we had got in the rest of the hospitals. In those places, nobody seemed to have heard of him; here everybody seemed to!

"Are you a medical student?" the girl at the reception – where I enquired first – asked me as soon as I had put my question to her. When I shook my head, she asked me once more: "Journalist?"

"No," I said shaking my head again; I was getting puzzled. "I am just searching for someone, a friend of mine," I told her.

"A girl actually. A twenty-six year old girl. She's disappeared… and we think this… this golden haired guy may know something about it. Is he here?"

The receptionist nodded. "Yes, of course. He was admitted on the 21st. A foreigner from Sweden. People keep coming to see him. Doctors and journalists both. Students too, often medical students. They look like you. That's why I asked if you were a medical student."

My heart sank. He was here. Hrithik was here. We had finally found him. I put on as big a smile on my face as I could and turned to Maahi to flash her a sign of victory. She smiled back but she wasn't as happy as I had expected her to be. In fact, she didn't look happy at all. I didn't understand her sometimes.

I turned back to the receptionist. I had to go on. "Do you know anything about the girl too?" I asked her.

"Girl?"

"Yes. The girl I just told you about. The friend I am looking for. A twenty-six year old pretty girl. Shall I give you a description? She may also have been brought to the hospital around the same time. I will be grateful if you can please check."

The receptionist frowned. "You are saying your friend came here with Mr Gulbandsen?"

"Gulbandsen?"

"Not Gulbandsen, *Gulbrandsen*. Gustav Gulbrandsen," the girl repeats the name. "That's what the police say is the name of the Swedish man. You are saying she came with him?"

"Not *came* with him. She may have been admitted with him. And if not exactly with him… around that time. Say between 19th to 22nd July. Could you please check?"

"A twenty-six year old girl?"

"Yes please. It's very important!"

The receptionist nodded, and then after asking for my name and where I had come from and a brief description of Maahi, she picked up the phone to dial someone. I turned to Maahi to…

But she wasn't there behind me! In fact, when I looked around, I couldn't see her anywhere in the lobby either! She had disappeared again.

I quickly walked away from the reception desk to glance into the corridors that led away from the lobby, but she wasn't in them. I focused. There were three more exits from the lobby: the door behind us through which we had come in, a lift on the right hand wall of the lobby, and a glass door to the left of the lift that you could see led to a staircase beyond. Now she couldn't have gone back the way we came in without telling me – that didn't make sense – but both the staircase and the lift were possibilities. I was standing close to the lift wondering what to do when the receptionist yelled my name from her desk: "Mr Mittal?"

"Yes!" I ran back to the reception.

"I am sorry… but no girl of twenty-six was admitted here between 19th to 22nd.

"No girl?"

"No."

"She… err… may have died here. Are you sure—"

"Died?"

"Yes," I said. "We have been unable to find the girl Maa… Manisha since the twentieth. There is no trace of her anywhere. No information at all. That's very unlike her. That's why unfortunately we are fearing the worst."

"I am sorry… but we're sure. No one matching your friend's description was admitted here in that time."

"Okay," I said, wondering what to do next. Where had Maahi disappeared to? Had she…

There was only one thing that I could do. "Can I know which room is Mr Gulbrandsen in?" I asked the receptionist. "And what's happened to him?"

"Mr Gulbrandsen?"

"Yes. I would like to talk to him."

"Talk to Mr Gulbrandsen? But—"

"Please. I have to find out about my friend. We think he may have been the last person who saw her. He may know something. It's critical that I talk to him."

The girl frowned. "You don't know then?"

My heart jumped. "Know what?" I paused. "Is he... dead?"

"Dead? No, not dead. He is alive. But he is in no condition to talk. Mr Gulbrandsen," the girl pronounced, "has been in a coma since the time he was admitted."

MAAHI:

The girl at the reception desk thinks for some reason we are medical students or journalists, but it seems we have finally found the golden haired man. He is Swedish.

Well, it explains the strange language of my dreams. But if that's true, how did I before my death fall in love with a Swedish man?

Pretending to be happy, Veeru turns to me and flashes the victory sign with a smile. I smile back. We are both pretending to be happy.

Veeru frowns. Am I not acting well enough? I guess so; it's difficult to pretend to the guy you love that you are in love with someone else. Then Veeru turns back and asks the receptionist about me – whether a girl of twenty-six was also admitted around the time the Swedish man was.

I am focused on what the receptionist is going to say when something makes me look to my right. It's the lift. As it closes full of people, I think I see the Marquis again! Standing at the back! I can't see his face clearly, but the clothes as always are difficult to miss. Am I hallucinating again or is it really the Marquis?

This time – if it's really him – I decide I am not going to let him give me the slip. The lift goes up before I have any chance of getting in it, but there are stairs on the left. I run to them as the receptionist reveals to Veeru the Swedish man's name which I hear to be Mr Gulbadan... something.

I am confused. Gulbadan? That sounds anything but Swedish! In fact, Gulbadan is a common Urdu name for girls and means someone who has a body as soft and fragrant as a flower. Anyway, I run after the Marquis; I can worry about the name later.

I climb the stairs, reach the first floor, and glance in the corridor left and right. No Marquis anywhere. I run on to the second floor. The same result. Third floor. Not here either. But on the fourth floor, I finally see the Marquis enter a room outside which a policeman stands guard. It's the fourth room on the right.

I sprint to the room as the policeman gets a call and starts talking on the phone. My eyes are searching for the Marquis as I enter the room. A golden haired handsome man in hospital clothes is lying on the bed, flat and still.

Hrithik!

The room is silent except for a periodic beep. Hrithik seems to be in a deep sleep but looks fine otherwise. There are no visible injuries on him, no sign as if he was ever in an accident or got hurt in any fashion.

I am surprised. I remember the words of the Marquis.

Death is never so gentle, at least not to people who she leaves trapped. Forget accident. How come you look as if... as if you never died at all?

I look closely at Hrithik; yes, the words of Marquis apply to him too. If not for the fact that he is lying on a hospital bed, no one would say there was anything wrong with him. He looks as if he is sleeping soundly, that's all.

Once again, I desperately wish the Marquis was here. To explain all this, to answer my questions. But where the hell is he?

I look around minutely. It's a small room with a smaller attached bathroom, but there's no trace of the Marquis in either rooms. He's disappeared again. For the second time.

VEERU:

Hrithik was in a coma! It made sense. The accident – He must have been in an accident that sent him into a coma.

But why wasn't Maahi found as well? She must have been in the accident too. She should have been brought here to the hospital too. Why wasn't someone of her description to be found in the records?

I felt flustered. There was no end to strangeness in this case. Had we, of all the coincidences in the world, managed to find the wrong golden haired man? It seemed almost impossible! And yet...

"How did Mr Gulbrandsen go into a coma?" I asked the receptionist. "Was it in an accident?"

Before she could answer me, the receptionist got another call. As she answered it, she kept glancing at me with interest. In the end, she nodded heavily to the speaker on the other side and after putting down the phone, told me: "Mr Mittal, I have a request for you."

Request? I was surprised. "Yes?"

"You will have to wait here for some time. Someone wants to talk to you."

While she said she was making a request, her tone didn't suggest a feeling of request.

"Who wants to talk to me?"

She hesitated. "I don't exactly know. A person from the police department."

"The police?"

"Yes."

"Why?"

"I don't know. It's about Mr Gulbrandsen. I am just following orders. I have been told to ask you to wait here."

She kept glancing towards the lift as she said this.

I was getting anxious. Why did the police want to talk to me? Was that in some way connected to the disappearance of Maahi? Had this Gulbrandsen dude something to do with it?

My earlier apprehensions returned. I remember I had suspected such a thing in the very beginning though Asmi ma'am had said 'no'.

Where was Maahi? I had to talk to her. Maybe stop her from seeing Gulbrandsen if that's what she had gone to do. I was suddenly very worried. A question had struck me: even if Maahi had been deeply in love with Gulbrandsen, assuming even that, would she still find the oblivion if Gulbrandsen himself was somehow responsible for her death and those memories flooded her on seeing him? I wasn't sure, but in that case I doubted very much of her finding the oblivion.

In fact, the effect on her could be just the opposite. The intense pain of betrayal may trap her, ground her here even more!

I had to find Maahi and stop her, hoping it wasn't already too late.

"I want to see Mr Gulbrandsen once before I meet anyone else," I told the receptionist urgently. "I want to confirm he is indeed the man I am searching for. If my friend was not admitted at the same time, he may not be the person we are trying to find. Which room is he in?"

But the receptionist was insistent as she glanced towards the lift again. "I am sorry Mr Mittal but I have been asked to tell you to wait here till the police come," she answered. "Please."

It was clear she wasn't going to tell me where Gulbrandsen was; I would have to find out for myself. I wanted to do that before I met the policeperson who must be coming down by the lift. So leaving the reception behind, I started walking swiftly towards the stairs to the left of the lift when the receptionist called me from behind.

"Mr Mittal!"

I ignored her call and kept going towards the staircase when she called my name again, this time yelling it sharply.

"Mr Mittal! Please STOP!"

A number of people in the reception were beginning to stare at me. A hospital attendant in white on my right stood alert as if ready – on a signal – to move on me. The situation looked tensed and I was going to break into a run when the door of the lift opened. A policeman in khaki was the first person to walk out of it, coming to a stop metres ahead of me.

Immediately the receptionist yelled something at him in Tamil while pointing a finger at me.

The policeman moved towards me and blocked my way. "Mr Mittal?"

I had no choice but to stop. He was a burly chap close to five feet ten. "Yes."

"Where are you going? Didn't the receptionist ask you to wait?"

"I want to see Mr Gulbrandsen immediately."

"Why?"

I frowned as if annoyed and in a stern tone said, "I have told the receptionist why. Doesn't she understand? One of my woman friends is missing and I was informed she was last seen with a golden haired man. I am told Mr Gulbrandsen is also golden haired and I want to check if Mr Gulbrandsen is really the person I am looking for. I have told that to her at least five times!"

"Mr Gulbrandsen can't talk to you. He is in a coma."

I nodded. "I was also told that. But that doesn't matter. I just want to have a look at him and see if the other description I was given of the golden haired man matches with him."

"What other description?"

"May I know why am I being asked so many questions?"

The policeman frowned at me for a few seconds. I guess I was being assessed. Then he smiled and said: "I assure you that you can see Mr Gulbrandsen later. That won't be a problem. But my senior Sub-Inspector Muralidharan wants to meet you first. He is coming from Kalapet station and he will be here soon... in about twenty minutes. He will answer all your questions. And you can see Mr Gulbrandsen after your meeting with

Muralidharan sir. Till that time, I am sorry but you will need to wait with me here."

"But why?"

"As I said, Muralidharan sir will answer all your questions. It's just a formality. Please be calm till then."

I realized I had no choice but to follow his order; it was an order even if couched in polite terms. Alone, I had no hope of finding Maahi or Gulbrandsen in a short time in this large hospital; and trying to do that by disobeying the policeman would most likely get me in police restraint and worsen matters. So I just did what he said.

Where was Maahi? God, please let her not find Gulbrandsen, let her come back here.

I was made to sit with Constable Jayakumar (that was the policeman's name) on a plastic bench in the lobby while we waited for Inspector Muralidharan. As the minutes passed, I kept looking at the staircase and the lift, hoping Maahi would show up. But she didn't come. Where was she?

After about half an hour, the inspector turned up. A physical contrast to Constable Jayakumar, he was a short but lean man with keen eyes and a weather-beaten face. He surveyed me with interest before asking me in a deadpan voice: "First time in Pondicherry, Mr Mittal?"

I nodded. "I—"

"I am SI Muralidharan. Jayakumar told me you are in a hurry to see Mr Gulbrandsen," he went on meaningfully. "Sorry to make you wait. But I need to ask you a few questions and then you can see whomever you want."

"Can you please tell me first why am I being made to answer these questions?" I replied to him with a touch of asperity. "What's the issue?"

"Yes, I will tell you," he said nodding. "Shortly. You look quite young. Aren't you?"

"I am twenty-five."

"I am thirty-seven. Twelve years older. And I can tell you patience is a very good thing. Let's sit down first." He smiled for the first time as we sat down next to each other. "Where are you from, Veerupakshya? That's your first name right?"

I nodded. "Yes, it is. I am from Bangalore."

"You have lived there your whole life?"

I shook my head. "No. Originally, I am from Ujjain. I shifted to Bangalore seven years ago to do my engineering, and after that my job."

"Ujjain is… MP right?"

I nodded. "Yes. It's very close to Indore."

"Your parents still live there?"

"Yes. And my father is a doctor and my mother is a housewife," I went on anticipating the next question. "I also have two siblings. An elder sister and a younger brother. Elder sister's a doctor, married and settled in Kolkata. Younger brother is studying to be a dentist in Pune."

"Very educated family," the inspector said nodding with approval. "Don't you also have a Jyotirlinga in Ujjain?"

"Yes. Mahakaleshwar."

"Have you been there?"

"Yes. Quite a few times."

"Do you believe in God Shiva?"

I was surprised. "My name itself is another name for Shiva. Why are you asking these questions? What has that anything to do with Mr Gulbrandsen?"

"That doesn't answer my question Veerupakshya. Do you believe in God Shiva?"

This irritated me. Maahi was in bloody trouble and I was being questioned whether I believed in God! I clenched my teeth. "You can call me Veeru. And I believe in Saguna Brahmana." Let him take that.

He frowned. "What?"

"Saguna Brahmana." It was my turn to smile a patronizing smile. "You should read the Vedanta. It's supposed to be the basis of our religion."

I guess I was being unnecessarily cocky and that was not wise, but Maahi was still missing and I was worried and angry. This was not a time to quiz me on my religious beliefs, for god's sake!

Mr Murali's smile disappeared. "So you don't believe in God Shiva?"

"I guess I do. When I say I believe in India, it automatically means I believe in Madhya Pradesh and Pondicherry, and other states too. It's like someone asking you if you are a Tamilian and you replying instead that you are an Indian or someone asking you if you are an Indian and you replying instead that you are a human being. If you are a human being, you can be Indian or Australian or whatever... being a human-being is more important. Shiva-Saguna Brahmana is a similar analogy."

The inspector nodded. "Interesting...What do you do in Bangalore?" he finally and mercifully moved on from my religious beliefs.

"I have started an e-Commerce company with my friend Jerry Rajeshwaran. He belongs to Kottayam in Kerala. We sell clothes, accessories, toys and baby products."

"What's the name of the company?"

"Company name is Arctic Bear Technologies. We are a registered company. And our website name is shoppingmuni. com. You can check on Google."

"So you are a capitalist?"

"What?" Was the man off his head or something?

"You run a business. So you must believe in capitalism."

"I and my friend are chasing capital right now for our company. So I guess, yes I do."

"Have you got the capital?"

"We are in the process. We are talking to investors."

"What kind of investors?"

"HNIs… angel funds. There are different groups. Bangalore group, Mumbai group, Chennai group. Typically these are high net-worth people who come together to fund start-ups. You can find them on Google. We are talking to them."

"And you haven't got the money till now?"

"No, not yet."

"How do you live then? Where do you get your money from? From parents?"

"*Not parents.*" I emphasized the words. Idiot! "We do freelance jobs. I am a freelance mobile application designer. Jerry does software architecture consulting. We pool in the money."

"And that pays you enough?"

Ok. So he wanted to know about my finances and money sources. No problem. "To sustain ourselves… yes."

"Why have you come to Pondicherry?"

Now this was a tricky one. The police couldn't be told the lies I had told the receptionist girl or others; they were likely to find it extremely odd and suspicious if I told them I had come searching for a girl who I didn't even know the name of. So for Inspector Muralidharan, I had cooked up a story that largely matched with the one I had narrated to the receptionist and yet explained why I knew nothing about Maahi. The only trouble was that making the story credible required the help of Asmi ma'am. But though I had tried her number while sitting with Constable Jayakumar, her phone was coming switched off. I had decided as soon as I could reach her, I will tell ma'am my story and ask her to help me.

"I came here searching for a girl," I told Inspector Muralidharan.

"What girl?"

"I don't know her name. I only know that she was in an accident here along with a golden haired man."

The inspector frowned. "What?"

"See… it's like this. We have a mentor for our start-up. Mentor means—"

I was interrupted curtly. "I know what a mentor is," the inspector barked.

"Okay. We have a mentor Asmita Deb Burman, a professor of Indian Institute of Science, Bangalore. You may have heard of IISc Bangalore?"

"Yes, I have."

"Great. So, on 21st evening, my mentor Professor Deb Burman received a call on her landline from an unknown number. It was a girl and she had called a wrong number. Said she was in a bad shape after an accident and didn't have the capacity to call another number, so she pleaded with ma'am to listen to her. Ma'am listened, of course. The girl said she was speaking from Pondicherry and she had been in an accident with her golden haired boyfriend and they needed help immediately. In between she also mentioned she was twenty-six. The phone got cut before the girl could say more. Ma'am didn't know what to do after that. She is anyway an old, half-blind lady and moves around with the help of a walking stick. Because she is old and half-blind and a little lost most of the times, quite like some old professors… I mean a little helpless in practical matters… we help her now and then with things. So a few days ago she shared the story with us and asked us what she should do. Obviously, it was too late to do anything concrete. But I offered to come here and do a search of the hospitals. Find out what had happened and whether help had reached the unfortunate couple in time. It was more to put ma'am's heart at ease than anything else. She's a kind and helpful lady and was feeling very guilty because she hadn't known what to do. Very upset with herself. We don't like to see her unhappy, so we offered to help. I thought hopefully I would find everything was okay." I shrugged. "I guess I had hoped for too much."

I chuckled inside as I told the inspector these pack of lies. Especially, to call Asmi ma'am lost and helpless was like calling a tigress vegetarian!

After a brief silence, the inspector said sceptically: "So you mean to say you came here to search for a girl you don't know anything about?"

"That's right."

"Not even her name?"

"No. Nothing… except that she was twenty-six years old and had a golden haired boyfriend."

I guess I had just told the biggest lie of my life. And I hated it.

But where was Maahi? Where was the actual girl about whom I knew nothing… and yet felt as if I knew everything? I was getting scared now and I just wanted to start searching for her. More than an hour had passed since she had disappeared.

And then another thought came to my mind, an idea that I had not considered in the past hour since I had assumed that Gulbrandsen was somehow involved in Maahi's death. But what if I had made a wrong assumption – what if Gulbrandsen had nothing to do with Maahi's death? Or what if despite the assumption being right, while I sat here answering petty or nonsensical questions of the inspector, Maahi had found her Hrithik and not remembered anything and found the oblivion? Suddenly – like that girl Olivia? What if Maahi was already…

"Can I talk to your mentor?"

A sharp pain gripped my heart.

"Hello! Mr Mittal?"

It had happened. It must have happened. That's why she hadn't come. While I was sitting here. I…

"*Veeru*!!"

"I am sorry. Yes?"

"What happened? What are you thinking?"

Thinking? I swallowed. What am I thinking? Maahi was perhaps gone. "I… I am sorry. I was trying to remember if there was anything else Professor Deb Burman told us."

"Can I talk to the professor sometime?"

"Yes, you can. I will give you her number. It's 9—"

"We will take that later. Let's get back to your story. Did the girl tell your mentor anything else? For example how the accident happened? Anything?"

The girl I loved was gone. I shook my head. "Nothing."

"Are you okay? You look upset. What happened?"

"Nothing. Nothing happened." Gone forever. My eyes were beginning to water. I had to control myself. "Can I go now?"

"Don't you want to know why we are asking you these questions?"

I nodded. No, I don't want to know. I just want to go. It was over. Everything. Please let me go.

"Tell me."

"Good! It will interest you."

Interest me? I wanted to laugh. I wanted to cry. I wanted to smash things. I sit here talking to you while the girl I loved went away. Forever.

"Sure. Tell me."

"You see... we are also trying to find the girl you are trying to find. Actually, it's the strangest case I have handled in my life."

MAAHI:

I sit next to Hrithik. I know probably nothing is going to happen, yet I keep sitting. There is a saying in Urdu: *Ummeed pe duniya qayam hai* - the world rests on hope.

And yet I think to myself, what am I hoping for anyway? Am I in any hurry to go? Do I want to go at all? The answer definitely is a 'no', isn't it? I guess I sit here just because as a ghost I am supposed to want the oblivion. The way we men and women are supposed to want heaven. I mean say you really find God after running after him for years – is this what you feel: that you never really wanted him? That you were chasing a mirage all the time? That even sitting beside him, as he sleeps, is a mistake? Why am I here?

Hrithik sleeps deeply, a milky fair man with hair of gold dressed in a spotless attire of white. His head is straight, his arms are straight and his legs are straight. Not even a hint of crookedness anywhere. And there are the gentle, almost imperceptible, undulations of the breast. He looks as if he is doing yoga. As if a Buddha is sleeping. Unbothered, untouched. Serene, pure. As if nothing has ever happened to him, and nothing will ever happen to him.

Ma'am had said the moment I see him, I would have a powerful desire to embrace him and kiss him. I guess ma'am was wrong. I don't recognize him. I don't feel anything.

After a long time, I get up. It's clear I will have to wait longer for the oblivion. I will have to be satisfied with being a wandering ghost for now. A wanderer like the Marquis. I wish I could find him.

It's time. Time to say goodbye to my real Hrithik. Veeru. Even if I can't actually touch him, before I go I want to fold him in my arms once. Kiss him.

But my feet feel like lead. I am tired again. I don't want to go down. I don't want to walk. I don't want to wander. I am tired. I don't want to be. I want to sleep like Hrithik. Not feel anything. Disappear. Maybe oblivion would have been better than this tiredness, this pain.

I don't want to leave Veeru.

I sit down at the door. The policeman has left. I sob. I sob like only a ghost can. Without tears.

I get up after some time. Sobbing is useless. Veeru needs me to go.

I start walking. Suddenly, I feel a force. Something is pulling me back gently. I look behind. There is nothing. Just the long silent corridor.

The pull again. It was stronger now, much stronger! I almost slipped!

Is it the oblivion? I don't understand. I am out of the room. I can't even see Hrithik! And there is no feeling of intensity, of joy, of serenity, of beauty like what the Marquis had described. There is no music, there is no sky.

Instead I am in a corridor. I am enclosed by concrete. I am tired. I am angry. I am unhappy. This is not fair. I…

The pull again! It catches me by surprise and drags me back almost a metre!

Veeru! But I have to meet Veeru! Say thanks! Embrace him! Kiss him! One last time. Not without that. I can't go without that!

I focus and teleport myself to the reception. I am struggling against the pull now. It's getting stronger and stronger. And continuous! Where is Veeru?

I look around. He is sitting with two policemen at the far side of the room. He is turned towards the policemen. His back is to me.

I try to teleport again. But I can't. I struggle hard. But I am rooted to the ground. It's impossible to move.

I try to yell. My tongue has frozen. I can't make any sound. What's happening? Please let me go. One last time.

I struggle wildly. I wave my arms. Veeru, please look back. No one else can see me. Please.

Veeru… look back!

I grit my teeth and give it my all one last time.

I have succeeded! The pull has lessened. I focus swiftly on teleporting. I close my eyes. But…

It returns. And it's stronger.

I can't struggle against it any more. I am sorry. Veeru, I am sorry. I am tired. It's far stronger than me. I give up.

I let go and at once I skid backwards. I gather speed. I see the Marquis staring at me as I am pulled through a wall out of the hall. *Marquis!* I yell. I am surprised but I can't stop. I am rushing through a flurry of rooms and things and walls. I don't understand. What happened? Why the Marquis?

Everything's confusing. Everything blurs and darkens. I am a train shooting through a dark tunnel with intermittent lights. I am something hurtling through nothing. I am nothing hurtling through nothing.

I come to a sudden bone wrenching stop. As if I have hit a wall of emptiness. I fall through emptiness. I fall and fall. And fall.

I close my eyes.

To Be Continued…